Letters · from

ATLANTIS

ROBERT

SILVERBERG

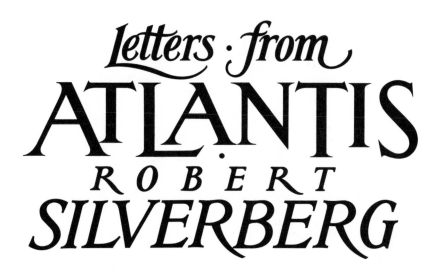

Letters · from ATLANTIS
ROBERT SILVERBERG

illustrated by
ROBERT GOULD

A Byron Preiss Book

Atheneum 1990 New York

Collier Macmillan Canada
Toronto

Maxwell Macmillan International Publishing Group
New York   Oxford   Singapore   Sydney

LETTERS FROM ATLANTIS
Dragonflight Books

LETTERS FROM ATLANTIS Copyright © 1990 by Byron Preiss Visual
Publications, Inc.
Text copyright © 1990 by Agberg, Ltd.
Illustrations copyright © 1990 Byron Preiss Visual
Publications, Inc.

Cover painting and design by Robert Gould
Interior book design by Robert Gould and Paula Keller
Book edited by Byron Preiss

Special thanks to Jonathan Lanman, David Keller,
and Alice Alfonsi

Library of Congress Cataloging-in-Publication Data

Silverberg, Robert.
Letters from Atlantis/by Robert Silverberg; illustrated by Robert Gould.—1st ed.
p. cm.
Summary: While his body remains in deep sleep, Roy transfers his mind into the
mind of a royal prince living in Atlantis 180 centuries ago.
ISBN 0-689-31570-8
[1. Time travel—Fiction. 2. Atlantis—Fiction. 3. Science fiction.]
I. Gould, Robert, ill. II. Title.
PZ7.S5858Le 1990
[Fic]—dc20
90-562
CIP
AC

Atheneum
Macmillan Publishing Company
866 Third Avenue, New York, NY 10022

Collier Macmillan Canada, Inc.
1200 Eglinton Avenue East
Suite 200
Don Mills, Ontario M3C 3N1
First Edition
Printed in the United States of America
10 9 8 7 6 5 4 3 2 1

Books in the Dragonlight Series

LETTERS FROM ATLANTIS
by Robert Silverberg

THE DREAMING PLACE
by Charles de Lint

. . . it waits for that serene moment when the brain is just in the apt condition, and ready to *switch on the other memory*, as one switches on the electric light with a turn of the switch. . . .

—Kenneth Grahame

. . . now in the island of Atlantis there was a great and wonderful empire, which had rule over the whole island and several others, as well as over part of the continent; and, besides these, they subjected the parts of Libya within the Columns of Heracles as far as Egypt, and of Europe as far as Tyrrhenia. . . . But there occurred violent earthquakes and floods, and in a single day and night of rain the island of Atlantis disappeared, and was sunk beneath the sea.

—Plato: *Timaeus*

□ O N E □

THE PRINCE IS SLEEPING NOW. Dreaming, no doubt, of the green and golden island of Athilan, its marble palaces, its shining temples. All unknown to him, I have borrowed his body—his good strong right arm—to write this letter for me.

So:

From somewhere in what I think is Brittany or Normandy, on what I think and assume is Christmas Eve in the year 18,862 B.C., greetings and merry Christmas, Lora!

(Will this ever reach you, out there in the frosty eastern land that will someday be Poland or Russia? Less than a fifty-fifty chance, I suppose, even though you're right here in the same prehistoric year I am. But a whole continent separates us. With transportation what it is here, it's almost like being in different worlds.

I'll cause the Prince to slip it into the regular diplomatic pouch that leaves next week, and the royal Athilantan courier will take it with him when he sets out across the tundra to the trading post where you're supposed to be stationed. With any luck you'll actually be there, and whoever you're riding in will be someone who routinely has access to the royal documents that the courier brings. Considering that I'm writing this in English, he won't have the remotest notion of what it's all about. But you will, looking at it through his eyes. And maybe you'll even be able to write back to me. My God, that would be wonderful, getting a letter from you! We've only been apart a little while and already it seems like forever.)

I suspect that the chances of my actually working out any sort of regular communication with you back here—or any communication at all, really—are very very slim. But I can try, anyway. And at the very least, setting down these accounts of what I've been experiencing here ought to provide me with a good way of bringing it all into clearer focus. Which should help me make better sense and order out of it when I'm home again in our own era and undergoing debriefing.

This is the seventh day of the mission. So far everything's moving along pretty well.

First there was the time-hop trauma to deal with, of course. That was a stunner, though actually not as bad as I was expecting; but naturally I was expecting the worst. This is such a big jump we've made— the biggest jump either of us has ever done, by far. During the training period the most I ever did was something like ninety years. This is a jump of *one hundred eighty centuries.* So I figured I'd come slamming into the Prince's mind behind a head of steam strong enough to knock me cold for a week. And in fact it was pretty rough, let me tell you.

The tuning was perfect. Of course the purpose of all the preliminary time-search scouting work was to locate a member of the royal family for me to use as my host. And they managed to land me right in the mind of nobody less than the heir to the throne himself!

I won't ever forget the moment of landing, which felt to me the way I'd expect to feel when hitting the water after a very clumsy dive made from a very high diving board. There was pain, real pain, a lot of it. It would have knocked the breath out of me if there had been any breath in me in the first place.

Then came the total strangeness of that wild moment when the minds are fusing, which you know all too well yourself—that time when you can't really tell whether you're *you* any more or somebody else—and then I blanked out.

So did the Prince, evidently.

We were unconscious for perhaps a day and a half, possibly a little more. That's why I'm not sure whether this is really Christmas Eve. Once I came to, and had made enough linguistic connections to be able to understand what I was hearing, I tried to figure out how long the Prince and I had been under, going by some of the things that the courtiers were saying to him:

"We rejoice, Highness, that the darkness has ended for you."

"Two days and a night did we pray, Highness! Two days and a night you were gone from us!"

But it hadn't been quite as long as that. As you've probably discovered yourself by now, their system of days and weeks isn't much like the one we use, what with a "day" being considered just the time between dawn and sunset, and the dark hours being called a "night," and the next biggest unit being a group of ten "days" and "nights" together, which works out to a five-day week on our scale, unless I still have it wrong. And two Athilantan days and a night would be a day and a half. But I do think this really is Christmas Eve, counting from the day we set out from Home Year and figuring up the total time that I believe has elapsed since then.

(A question, Lora: Is it really proper to regard this day as Christmas Eve, considering that we're currently living at a time thousands of years before Christ's birth? I suppose it is. We did set out from an A.D. Home Year, after all. But still the idea strikes me as a little peculiar. Then again, *everything* about this venture seems a little peculiar, starting with the fact that you and I have been converted into nothing more than nets of electrical energy and have been hurled thousands of years into the past, leaving our bodies behind in deepsleep. But telling myself that this is Christmas Eve makes it feel just a little homier for me here. God knows I need to have things feel a little homier right now. So do you, I imagine, out there in the frozen wastelands of the mammoth-hunter people.)

I have a very good link with the Prince's mind. I

can read his every thought, I can understand the things he says and the things that are said to him, I can monitor his heartbeat and his respiratory rate and the hormonal output of his glandular system. I am able to anticipate the movements of his body even before he consciously knows he's going to make those movements. I pick up impulses traveling from his brain to his muscles, and I feel the muscles getting ready to react. I could, whenever I choose, override his own conscious commands and get his body to do whatever I felt like having it do. Not that I'd do any such thing—not while he's awake and aware. I don't want him to start thinking that he's been possessed by a demon, even though that's essentially what has happened to him.

How does it feel, Lora, thinking of yourself as a demon? Not so good, eh? But that's what we really are. That's the truth, isn't it?

The Prince doesn't have the slightest suspicion, I'm sure, that he's been invaded this way, that an intruder from the distant future is inside him, wrapped around his entire nervous system like a blanket of undetectable mist.

I know that he felt me arriving. It wouldn't have been possible for him not to feel the impact of that. But he had no clear notion of what was actually happening.

"The fingertip of a god has touched my soul," he told his companions. "For a time I was thrown into darkness. The gods chose to touch me, and who can say why?"

Some kind of stroke, in other words. And then a day and a night and a day of unconsciousness.

Well, the gods work in mysterious ways. So far as anyone knows, the Prince has made a complete recovery from whatever it was that smote him. I remain hidden, crouching invisible within his mind, a mysterious web of electrical impulses safe from any Athilantan means of detection.

And now he sleeps. I can't read his dreams, of course—that layer of his mind is much too deep to reach—but his body is at peace, very relaxed. That's why I think he's dreaming of his homeland, the warm sweet isle of Athilan. Most likely he thinks he's lying in his own soft bed.

But he isn't.

A little while ago I picked him up and sleepwalked him over to his fine shining desk, made of rare and strange timber from the southern lands—something black that may be ebony inlaid with strips of several bright golden woods—and right now he's sitting upright, hard at work writing this letter for me. Taking dictation, so to speak. A royal prince, taking dictation. But how could he ever know that?

The only clue he could possibly have is the stiffness that's building up in his right arm and hand. The shape of the letters we use is very different from the Athilantan curlicues and spirals he's accustomed to, and his muscles are straining and cramping as he writes. When he wakes up, though, he'll never be able to guess why his arm is a little sore.

We're near the seacoast, getting ready to break camp and take ship for Athilan itself. The Athilantans have a fairly big outpost here, perhaps three or four hundred people. The name of the place seems to be

Thibarak. There are little primitive mainlander en-
campments scattered widely through the country-
side all around. The mainlanders, who come to
Thibarak to trade with the Athilantans, regard the
powerful island people virtually as gods. I imagine
that's true all over Europe, for as far as the Athilantan
empire reaches.

The landscape here is pretty grim and forbid-
ding, though I suppose nothing like the way it is
where you are in Naz Glesim. No glaciers here, no
ice-fields—the ice has all retreated to the north and
east by now—but the ground has a raw, scraped
look to it, bare and damp, rough and rocky. The
weather is very, very cold. I doubt that it's been
above freezing at all since I've been here, though the
days are bright and sunny. Still, it's evidently a lot
warmer than it was a few hundred years ago, or
than it is right now out where you are, which must
be still pretty much in the grip of the ice. We have
some birch and willow trees here, and a few pines.
I've seen occasional mammoths and bison, but not
many: the big Ice Age animals don't like these new
forests, and have wandered away to colder country
where the grazing is better.

The Prince's name is Ramifon Sigiliterimor
Septagimot Stolifax Blayl, which means, approxi-
mately, Beloved of the Gods and Light of the Universe. But nobody calls him that, because it would
be sacrilegious. I learned it by rummaging around in
the basement of his memory. His parents call him
Ram, which is short for all the rest. His brothers and
sisters call him Premianor Tisilan, which means First

of the Family. Everybody else calls him Stoy Thilayl, which means Your Highness.

He is eighteen years old, dark-haired and olive-skinned, and very strong, with enormous shoulders and forearms. He's shorter than he'd like to be, though—in fact, not very tall at all, even by Athilantan standards—and he's not too happy about that, though he knows it can't be helped. Generally he seems good-natured and very capable. Some day, if all goes well for him, he'll become Grand Darionis of the Island of Athilan. Or, in other words, King of Atlantis.

I wonder what he'd think if he knew that his magnificent island of Athilan, which has built such a glorious empire and rules the entire Ice Age world, is doomed to be destroyed in another few hundred years. So thoroughly destroyed, indeed, that the people of future ages will come to think of its very existence as nothing more than a pretty myth.

For that matter, I wonder how he'd react if he were to learn that the people of future ages are sending observers back across a gulf of nearly twenty-one thousand years to find out something about this Athilantan Empire, and that one of them is currently sitting right inside his own mind.

Well, I'm not likely to discover what he would make of that. The last thing I'm going to do is tap the Prince on the shoulder and say, "Hi, Prince, guess who's here!"

I hope that everything is fine for you out in the frozen hinterlands. I think of you all the time and miss you more than is really good for me. Write to

me, if you can. Tell me everything that's happening to you. Everything!
      More later.
      Much love—

—Roy

□ T W O □

F OUR DAYS HAVE GONE BY SINCE MY LAST.

I mean four of our 24-hour days, not the half-day "days" that the Athilantans use. We're still here on this barren, frosty coast. The Athilantan ships are waiting in Thibarak harbor to take us to the island, but there are all sorts of rites and rituals that have to be performed first. Mainlander people in startling numbers—there must be thousands of them—have turned up to bid farewell to the Prince as he makes ready to set out for home. I suppose it isn't a common thing to have a prince of the royal blood visiting here. And so every day we have bonfires blazing, bulls being sacrificed, chanting going on and on. Prince Ram presides over it with terrific aplomb. It's plain that he's been raised from childhood to rule the empire, and he knows exactly what needs to be done.

But though I haven't been able to budge yet from my starting point, this place, provincial as it is,

□ 11

has plenty of fascination of its own. Maybe it isn't glittering wonderful Atlantis, but it's the *past*, Lora, the remote and weird prehistoric past!

It's astonishing just being here. Every minute brings something new. I want to turn to you and say, "Look at that, Lora! Isn't that incredible?" But of course you aren't here. You're way over there in eastern Europe. If only we could have made this trip together! (I know, I know, we *are* together, sort of. But I'm here and you're there, instead of our both being in the same place. And don't bother telling me that it would be unnecessary duplication of resources to send two observers to the same place as well as the same time. I know all that. I still wish you were here, close enough for me to talk to every day.)

But since you aren't, I'll tell you what I'm learning. And one of these days maybe I'll be lucky enough to hear what you've been up to, too.

The difference between the Athilantans and the mainlanders is enormous. I don't just mean the cultural difference, which is even wider than the gap, say, between the Romans of Caesar's day and the savages who lived in the forests of Germany and France. That was Iron Age versus Bronze Age; this is Iron Age versus Stone Age. But I mean the physical difference. You must be seeing it, too. They're two different types of people altogether.

Correct me if I'm wrong, but my impression is that the mainlanders here at Thibarak are the people that archaeologists call the Solutreans, who lived in this part of Europe a couple of thousand years after Cro-Magnon times. These Solutreans are tall, slender, fair-haired people with a sort of Viking look about them. They wear leather clothes very finely stitched together, and they use stone tools that look pretty elegant to me, long and thin and tapering, with a lot of fine little chip-strokes around the edges. Mostly they make their homes in shallow caves or beneath shelters of overhanging rock, though I see from Prince Ram's mind that in the warmer seasons they also build little flimsy wickerwork huts for themselves.

The Athilantans are nothing remotely like them in any way.

The island folk tend to be much shorter and stockier than the mainlanders, with dark hair and somewhat swarthy skins. Their eyes are brown or black, never blue. It's basically a Mediterranean look, Greek or Spanish, and yet there's something not quite convincingly Greek or Spanish about them that I can't put my finger on. Their cheekbones have an oddly slanted look, their mouths are a little too wide, the shape of their heads is a little strange. Maybe you've noticed it too, even though there are only five or six Athilantans out there in Naz Glesim, and I have hundreds to observe here.

My theory, for what it's worth, is that the Athilantans actually are the ancestors of the Mediterranean folk of our Home Era, but modern Mediterranean people look a little different from Athilantans because of the changes that have taken place during all the thousands of years of evolution and interbreeding since the destruction of Athilan. I realize, though, that that's only a guess and may be very wide of the mark.

What amazes me most is how advanced the Athilantans are, technologically speaking, over the mainlanders. Atlantis really was a magical kingdom! It's almost unbelievable, when you stop to think about it—a wealthy and far-flung maritime empire that understands the use of iron and bronze, a civilization at least as advanced as those of Greece and Rome, way back here in the Upper Paleolithic Era!

How strange that archaeologists have never found any of their artifacts. No bronze swords or daggers mixed in with Cro-Magnon stone tools, none of their sculpture, no fragments of the buildings they erected on the mainland of Europe at outposts such as the ones you and I are currently at. Part of the answer, I guess, is that even though modern-world archaeologists have been digging up ancient ruins in a serious way for the past few hundred years they've still only scratched the surface of the buried remains of the ancient cultures and simply haven't had the good luck to come across any Athilantan artifacts so far. And maybe bronze daggers will rust beyond discovery in twenty thousand years, whereas stone tools last forever. But that can't be the whole explanation.

Well, I have a theory about that, too, Lora.

What if—after the fall of Athilan—the oppressed people of mainland Europe arose and systematically rounded up every last trace of their Athilantan masters, every weapon and tool and bit of sculpture they could find, and carried the whole business out to sea and dumped it all? Every scrap. Out of some tremendous vindictive urge they blotted the Athilantans from the face of the Earth. And twenty thousand years of ocean silt did the rest.

What do you think?

Sooner or later, time research will give us the answer. We can be pretty certain of that. We'll pinpoint the exact date of the destruction of Athilan and send observers into Europe to see what happened after that. But for the moment, I think my idea's as good as anything that's been suggested.

I have a lot of time to sit here thinking up these theories, right now. And I have to confess, despite what I said a little earlier, that I really am getting tired of this place. I want to get moving. I want to see Atlantis.

How tremendously frustrating it is to know that the royal ships are waiting in the harbor, ready to carry us off to that warm and beautiful and fabulous land out in the ocean, and instead I'm stuck in this chilly miserable place somewhere on the coast of France while the endless rituals and sacrifices are performed and rivers of bulls' blood run along the rocky ground. Prince Ram stands on top of a wicker-work tower, smiling and waving and scattering hand-fuls of grain to the groveling mainlanders. Imagine it, *grain,* in Paleolithic Europe, where farming isn't supposed to have been invented for another ten or fifteen thousand years! As the prince tosses the grain, long lines of the local folks keep coming on and on to snatch it up, more people than I ever would have guessed there were in the whole world at this time.

I really don't want to be here in this two-bit provincial trading post any longer. Yes, it's fascinating in its way, I suppose. But it's also cold and raw and primitive, and it isn't Atlantis. I want to see Atlantis. Lord, do I want to see Atlantis! It'll be just my luck if the whole place sinks into the sea before I get there. We aren't sure, after all, precisely when the final cataclysm is due to happen. It could even be next week, though I like to think there's more time than that. Nevertheless here I sit. Here I wait.

Miss you so very much.

Until next time—

—Roy

□THREE□

WRITTEN AT SEA. I'm embarrassed to report that I've already lost count of the days, but I'm sure that we are just past the turning of the year—going by the Home Era calendar, that is. By the Athilantan calendar too, for that matter, because I've learned that the Athilantans begin their year on the day of the winter solstice, our December 21. That makes sense: the day the sun begins its return, the day when the days begin to grow longer.

(If you've done a better job of keeping track of time than I have, Lora, can you help me out? When and if you answer this, give me a clue, in terms of the phases of the moon or something, to the exact date in Home Era time. Not knowing the exact calendar time right now doesn't matter all that much, but I can see that it could cause big problems for me as the time draws near to return to our own time. I shouldn't have messed up like this. Dumb of me, dumb, dumb, dumb!)

Anyway, I'll assume that by our own calendar today is January 3, 18,861 B.C. I can't be more than a day or two off. So: Happy New Year, Lora! (Give or take a day or two. . . .) Happy New Year! But it's really difficult to keep converting Athilantan days into our days, and really dumb to use a calendar that has no relevance whatever back here. I suspect that you're using the Athilantan calendar now, although you've most likely been keeping track of the Home Era time as well. Since I can't really be sure of the right Home Era date any more, I might as well switch over to the local system. And—well—by Athilantan reckoning, I see by Prince Ram's mind, this is Day 13 of the Month of New Light in the year of the Great River. So be it.

Starting over, then—

Day 13, New Light, Great River. Aboard the imperial Athilantan vessel *Lord of Day*, bound from Brittany toward the isle of Athilan!

You ought to see these ships, Lora! You wouldn't believe them for a moment.

What I expected, considering the general cultural level of these Athilantans as I've come to know it in the short while I've been here, was something along the lines of the Greek or Roman galley, with two or three banks of oars and maybe a sail. Or, maybe, a vessel more like a merchantman—you know, a pure sailing ship, square-rigged or possibly with a lateen sail.

Lora, this is some kind of steamship. I'm not kidding. A *steamship*. In the Paleolithic!

Unbelievable. Incomprehensible.

I said last time that the Athilantans were an Iron Age people living in Stone Age times. That was an understatement, by plenty. I hadn't had a chance yet to study my surroundings carefully enough. These people aren't simply on a cultural par with the Greeks or the Romans, as I used to think—no, they've got at least a nineteenth-century technology, and maybe something even more advanced than that. I wasn't able to see that on the mainland, and you probably can't see it out where you are. But this ship is an eye-opener.

I'm not sure that there are actual steam engines down below. For all I really know, the engine room is staffed by a team of sorcerers who keep giant turbines going round and round by uttering spells. Truth is, I don't know *what's* down there, and neither does Prince Ram. Princes don't need to bother with such technological details, apparently. I'd like to sleepwalk him down belowdecks so that I could have a look around, but I don't dare. Not until I'm completely sure that my control over his mind is good enough to keep him asleep as long as I want. I don't want him suddenly waking up and finding himself down in the engine room, where somebody of his high rank ordinarily has no reason to go. And then starting to wonder if there's something funny going on inside his brain.

This much I can tell you, though. The ship is big, as large as a good-sized yacht, long and tapering, with a flat stern and a very high keel. The hull is of metal: iron, probably, but for all I know these people may be capable of fabricating steel. You may balk at that idea, but just keep on reading.

There's a mast, a big one, but no sign of any rigging or lines. Either the mast has some sacred purpose or it's some kind of antenna, but it isn't used to support sails. There are also two funnels, or smokestacks. I never see any smoke coming out of them. I can feel a very light but steady vibration, as though engines of some sort are at work. That's all I know.

Oh, one other thing. *These people use electricity.*

I know, I know, I know. It sounds nutty. The first time I saw the lights coming on, I thought the Prince was hallucinating. Or else that I must be misreading the data, coming up with false sensory equivalents for what was passing through his mind. Or maybe *I* was the one who was hallucinating. I tell you, Lora, it hit me like an earthquake. I was rocked by it. Flustered, bewildered, disoriented. For a moment I wondered whether I could believe anything that I was perceiving. Maybe it was all equally cockeyed. Paleolithic *electricity?*

But I checked and doublechecked, and the signal was coming through clear and true from him to me. What I was perceiving was what Prince Ram was seeing, to the last decimal place. So it wasn't any fever dream. It was electric lighting, Lora. However incredible that sounds.

Where I was on the mainland, everything was lit by properly prehistoric-looking oil lamps, smelly and smoky, and no doubt it's the same out your way. But every corridor of this ship that I've seen so far, and every stateroom too, I suspect, has electric lights. I suppose they simply haven't bothered to set up generators in the mainland outposts, or maybe there's no ready supply of fuel for them there. But they must have some kind of generator aboard ship, cranking out the kilowatts just like at home.

The light-globes are big and awkward, and the light they give is harsh and glaring, but there's no question that it's electrical. I've seen Prince Ram turn the light in his cabin on and off by touching a plate in the wall.

With no effort whatsoever I could make myself believe that I'm aboard a twentieth-century vessel—a peculiar one, true, designed by someone from an obscure country who has invented the whole concept of the oceangoing ship from scratch without ever having seen one from Europe or the United States, but corresponding to them in all the important details. And yet I know that I'm back here at the tail end of the Ice Age, with woolly mammoths and shaggy rhinoceroses still wandering around where Paris and London will someday be.

Who are these Athilantans, anyway? How could they possibly have achieved all this, tens of thousands of years out of the normal human sequence of cultural evolution? It doesn't make any sense. Suddenly, in the midst of a world that still uses flint axes and choppers, for a society to spring up that has mastered metals, engineering, architecture, even electricity—it's crazy, Lora. I don't get it. The old myths said that the Atlanteans were a great people, but not that they were miracle-workers.

Well, let that be for now. I have plenty of other things to tell you.

I'm pretty sure now that the place we set out from was the coast of Brittany. We all knew in advance back at Home Era, when we began focusing on members of the ruling caste as my target, that important members of the royal family made regular inspection tours of the coastal provinces and that if they aimed me at the mind of one of the high princes I was just likely to come down in ancient France as in Athilan itself.

Certainly the stone tools that the mainlanders were using were the sort of things used in France at this time. And the harbor was a good one. Whether Thibarak was Cherbourg or Le Havre, I can't say; but unless I have my geography all cockeyed we have just sailed out through the English Channel—on the clear days it seemed to me I could see the English shore to the north—and now we are running far into the Atlantic, curving down past Portugal toward the mouth of the Mediterranean. Which is just where our archaeologists had decided was the most likely place for Atlantis to have been, of course—somewhere between the Canary Islands and the Azores.

The weather gets milder and warmer every day. Birds, soft breezes (even in the middle of an Ice Age winter!), drifting masses of seaweed. There is a lot of rain, virtually daily, but it's a gentle kind of rain and when the sun comes out afterward the rainbows are heartbreaking. Especially when I stop to think that Atlantis lies at the end of them.

Life aboard ship is—

Uh-oh—trouble—

*   *   *

Six or seven hours later, same day.

A narrow escape. I was using the Prince to write this letter, and I almost got caught.

Ram was in his stateroom, sitting in one of the hammocklike things that they use on this ship. I had him under trance, and I was telling you all about the weather at sea when suddenly his personal steward came in. To tidy up the room, I suppose.

It isn't the custom among the Athilantans to knock on doors. They make a kind of high whistling noise when they want to enter a room. I was so preoccupied with dictating my letter that I didn't even notice. So in walks the steward, and he sees the heir to the imperial throne sitting bolt upright in his hammock with a weird trance look on his face.

"Your Highness!" he says. And then, in real terror, "*Your Highness?!?*"

He rushes over, seizes the Prince, shakes him hard. Well, you can bet I broke contact with the Prince's mind right away. He snapped out of it and looked around in confusion and got angry with the steward for bothering him while he was trying to take a nap. That part went all right.

But I couldn't put the Prince back into trance until the steward had left the cabin. And the steward took just long enough to get out of there so that the Prince had time to look down at the sheet of vellum he was holding, and stare at the nonsensical marks scribbled all over it.

So when the steward finally was gone, there was Prince Ram sitting there, wide awake, holding a sheet of vellum in one hand and an ink-stylus in the other, and the vellum was covered with strange marks. Marks that were, in fact, a script that nobody on Earth is going to be able to understand for another good many thousands of years.

He was absolutely mystified. He held it up close to his eyes, turned it upside down, shook his head in bewilderment. And I heard his thought loud and clear:

—*What in the name of all the gods is THIS?*

Well, I put him back to sleep and tried to get down into his mind and eradicate all memory of what he had just seen. As you know, that isn't the easiest thing in the world to do. You poke around in your carrier's short-term memory, trying to blot out a particular incident, and if you're not really careful, you can blot out half a day of other stuff, or a whole week, or even start ripping up the basic memory framework before you realize what you're doing. I didn't want to leave him feeling like an amnesia victim. So I tiptoed around in his memory bank, slicing here and there, doing my best. I think I did the job as nicely as anybody could have; but when I was done, I wasn't entirely confident that I had completely cleaned things up.

I hid the letter. And then I hid myself, getting down into stasis and just sitting quietly in a subconscious corner of the Prince's brain all afternoon. I didn't try to make contact with his cerebral levels in any way whatever.

(That's the hardest thing of all to do, I think— when you have to lay low, sitting tight, doing nothing. After all, we aren't capable of going to sleep. And disembodied entities like us can't just head out for a long walk to kill the time. So there we sit, unable even to twitch. Like prisoners in a cage no bigger than a human brain, absolutely immobilized, counting off seconds and minutes for lack of anything else to do. It's maddening, isn't it? It's almost unbearable.)

I guess I could have used the time to prowl through the Prince's basic memory storage to pick up a little useful data about the Athilantan civilization, but I didn't dare. He might just be able to detect me poking around—a curious itchy feeling in his mind, let's say. I didn't want to arouse any more suspicions than I already had. And it seemed to me right then that there already was an odd new edge to the Prince's mind, a kind of prickly wariness.

I've seen that happen before. But on other occasions, when my carrier has been allowed to get an inkling of the real situation, it has passed in a few hours. Sure enough, that's what happened this time. Ram began to relax, the edge on his mind went away, he went about his princely duties as though nothing had occurred. And ten minutes ago he returned to his cabin to relax. I put him under trance and got this unfinished letter out of its hiding place.

What a strange business this is, hitchhiking through the past inside someone else's mind! I've done it a dozen different times now, and I'm still not fully used to the idea. I'm not sure I really like it very much—treating another human being as a mere vehicle, moving him this way and that for your own convenience, going through his most intimate thoughts and memories as though he were nothing more than software available for scanning. Sometimes it seems a little ugly. Like being a spy, in a way. What it amounts to is that nobody who ever lived has any secrets from us time-traveling, twenty-first century nosybodies.

On the other hand, since it's physically impossible for us to travel through time except as intangible electrical impulses, this is how we have to do it. And it does allow us to recapture all kinds of astounding knowledge that otherwise would have been lost forever in the bottomless sea of the past.

Anyway—picking up where I left off so many hours ago—

We are obviously moving into subtropical seas. Even in the Ice Age, it seems, the midsection of the world had pretty decent weather, much rainier than it is in Home Era but not particularly cold. There's a springtime tenderness in the air that everyone aboard ship is responding to. The Prince and his whole retinue have been on the chilly mainland more than a year, and they're as eager to get back to Athilan as I am to see it for the first time.

This afternoon the Prince was working on a report to his royal father about the current status of Athilantan trading posts on the mainland—evidently the thing that he was sent to Europe to investigate. There was a map open on his desk as he worked, and I was able to see the whole layout of the empire.

Incredible!

They've got outposts strung all along the southern half of Stone Age Europe as far east as Russia, and down into North Africa and the Middle East. Most of the trade is done by sea, but a network of roads links everything together inland. It's awesome how they have it all connected, couriers going back and forth over an elaborate network of highways. (No, I don't think they use automobiles—all I saw while I was in Brittany were chariots, some drawn by small, sturdy, fierce-looking horses, and some by what looked like enormous reindeer.)

And all this will be lost. All this will be totally forgotten, as though it had never been. The memory of it will survive only as fable and myth, which no one will really take seriously until the coming of the age of time exploration. It's heartbreaking to think about it.

The Athilantan highway system runs up as far as what I think is the middle of Germany, then zigs and zags through Central Europe, avoiding the most heavily glaciated areas. One of the roads goes straight to Naz Glesim, where you are, the easternmost outpost of the empire. It gave me a funny feeling to see that name on the map and know that you're there at this very moment.

Thibarak, the coastal trading post where I was, in Brittany, is a sort of headquarters for the imperial mainland operations—at least the Western European branch. Couriers go back and forth between Thibarak and Naz Glesim all the time, bearing directives from the home government and reports from the provincial governor. The trip takes a couple of months each way. I should be able to slip these letters into the diplomatic pouch, and if you really did make it into the mind of Provincial Governor Sippurilayl as they planned it when they did the preliminary time-search, you'll eventually get to read them. Or not, as the case may be. Try to arrange it so that Governor Sippurilayl sends letters back to Prince Ramifon Sigiliterimor. That way I'll see them sooner or later. Then, of course, we both will have to wipe out of our carriers' minds all memory of the strange messages in unknown gibberish that they keep getting from each other. But with practice that won't be too hard.

I think we'll reach Atlantis in another four days or so. At sundown the Prince was standing on the deck wearing only a light tunic and mantle, and soft warm breezes were blowing out of the south.

Poor Lora! You must be freezing your butt off out there on the barren Russian steppes while I sit here telling you about the sweet springlike weather we're enjoying. Well, I don't mean to rub it in, you know. It was just the luck of the toss that sent me to Atlantis and you to Naz Glesim, and I'm well aware that a mere matter of heads instead of tails and I'd be the one stuck in the back woods right now. And next trip it may be the other way around for us.

(A pity that they won't ever send us to the same locale when we make these jumps. I know, I know, they want to spread us out over the maximum territory. The best we can hope for is to go to the same era but in different geographical regions. Which I guess is better than nothing. As they told us when we volunteered for this, time travel works best when two people who have a strong emotional connection are sent out as a team. And they're right. Simply knowing that you're here—thousands of miles away, sure, but in the same *era*—gives me a warm, comfortable feeling. And that helps immensely in fending off the terrible isolation that would otherwise come with knowing that I'm so distant in time from everything and everyone that I care for. All the same, I'd like to be able to *see* you once in a while. I'd like to be able to *touch* you. I'd like to be able to—oh, well, never mind. At least I can write to you. And maybe one of these days the courier will get back from the eastern part of the empire and there'll be a letter from you to me.)

Meanwhile Atlantis gets closer every second.

Until then—give my regards to all my good friends in Naz Glesim, if there happen to be any, which I doubt.

Miss you miss you miss you miss you.

—Roy

□ FOUR □

DAY 27, MONTH OF NEW LIGHT, Year of the Great River—

Atlantis, Lora! I'm in Atlantis!

The island of Athilan, I should say. It came into iew in the middle of the night, while Prince Ram slept. There came a whistling at the door and they woke him up, because he had to perform the Ritual of Homecoming. We went out on deck. And then at last I saw it, gleaming in the moonlight right in front of us.

It's a lofty island, rising high out of the Western Atlantic. The great mountain in the middle, which is called Mount Balamoris, is as I think you know the volcano that sooner or later is going to blow this whole place to oblivion. Later rather than sooner, I profoundly hope. But obviously Mount Balamoris has been inactive for hundreds or even thousands of years, and a fantastic city has been built on its vast slopes and down along the broad plain that runs to the sea.

□ 31

What was on my mind as we made our final approach to Atlantis was the description of it that Plato gave in his dialog *Kritias*, which you and I studied while we were in training. That Atlantis was a "continent," rich and beautiful, with an abundance of trees and shrubs, flowers and fruits, animals both wild and tame, and precious minerals. And that the capital city, on the southern coast, was a huge metropolis, fifteen miles around, having the form of two circular strips of land divided by three wide canals, with great walls of stone, bridges, towers, and palaces. At the center of the city was a holy quarter within an enclosure of gold, where the temples were covered with gold and silver and their roofs were made of ivory.

I can hear you reminding me that nobody in modern times takes Plato's account seriously as history. Well, yes, I know that. I haven't forgotten that he wrote it around 355 B.C. and even he says that Atlantis had been destroyed 9,000 years earlier. Which means he can't possibly have any hard data about it, because 9,000 years before Plato's time Greece was deep in prehistoric darkness. I'm aware that it's been the general scholarly belief for a long time that Plato probably made the whole story up himself—that all it is is a fantasy, just a pleasant work of fiction.

But is it? I wonder. Now that I've had a look at Atlantis with my own eyes, I'm not so sure that Plato was simply making it all up from scratch.

One thing we know, thanks to time exploration, is that Atlantis actually existed. As recently as the twentieth century it was thought to be purely mythical. But no: we have proof now that a spectacularly great island-city really did exist in the middle of the Atlantic Ocean thousands of years before Plato's time, and that it really was destroyed by a gigantic cataclysm. So it certainly isn't beyond belief that memories of the place and its horrendous destruction might have passed into legend, or that tales of fabulous Atlantis could have been told and retold for generation after generation, across time immemorial. And some confused bits and scraps of those ancient legends might still have been circulating in the Mediterranean region at the time when Plato lived.

The strange thing is how much the real Atlantis, the place that I'm staring at even as I write this, actually does resemble the one that Plato described.

It isn't a continent, of course. It's a just a very large island, maybe the size of Borneo or Madagascar. But how can you tell, when you see some enormous landmass in front of you that stretches a vast distance out of sight in both directions, whether you're looking at a continental shore or simply a big island? Plato wasn't that far off the mark. Certainly Atlantis was much bigger than Great Britain or Cuba or Iceland.

He was wrong about other details. For example, the capitals's not on the southern shore. It's on the western one. But the city *does* have a circular layout, with huge walls made up of giant stone blocks laid one atop another. The masonry work was done with fantastic precision, too. It's absolutely perfect. There are waterways and bridges inside the walls, and splendid boulevards that no city on Earth could have equalled until modern times. Perhaps no city of modern Earth does.

And I tell you, Lora, this waterfront district right here is amazing. If you could only see it! There's a tremendous semicircular harbor with a massive quay of black granite faced with pink marble, and stone piers jutting far out into the water. All around me are Athilantan ships that have come in from all over the world, and right at this minute I'm watching them unloading what must be absolutely fabulous cargoes. Officials are checking everything out on shore, boxes and boxes full of precious metals and jewels, spices, furs, strange animals, rare woods.

Then, over to one side of the harbor, there's the Fountain of the Spheres, which shoots an enormous jet of water into the sky every quarter-hour. On the other side is the Temple of the Dolphins, a white marble structure that has the most incredibly pure, balanced design. Believe me, it makes the Parthenon itself look a little shoddy.

A broad street, the Street of Starwatchers, runs just back of the waterfront. At the head of the Street of Starwatchers there's an imposing domed tower, the Imperial Observatory, and just behind it begins a tremendous avenue, the Concourse of the Sky, which cuts through the city for miles, leading to—yes, a central zone of sacred buildings, just like Plato said, set on a sloping hill. The walls of the temples are covered with white marble, not Plato's silver and gold, but when the afternoon sun strikes them the entire city blazes with reflected light.

The city continues on the far side of the sacred zone, sprawling right up into the foothills of Mount Balamoris. Beyond are parks, farms, the mines where copper and iron and gold are found, and a huge forest preserve full of all manner of wild beasts, including a herd of elephants. I don't mean the woolly mammoths that are roaming around in Ice Age Europe out where you are, but plain old ordinary elephants, very much like the ones we can see in the zoo, except I think these are even bigger. They've got ears the size of tents.

The climate here is extremely gentle. Judging by the fact that night and day are just about equal in length even in midwinter, I'd say that Atlantis is located smack on the Tropic of Cancer, or else not very far north of it. There's a little rain just about every day, but it clears off fast and in a little while the sun is out again and everything's nice and warm. The air is mild and beautifully transparent, the sky is a delicate blue, and wherever you look you see flowers in bloom. It's hard to believe that at this very moment most of Europe and North America is buried under ice. Or that enormous shaggy shambling mammoths and rhinos are grazing in the places where our great cities are going to be built some time in the far future. Or that little bands of men clad in furs are out there trying to hunt them with crude weapons made out of stone.

No wonder shimmering memories of this place continued to glow in the minds of people like Plato thousands of years later. In every human tribe the wise old storytellers must have passed vivid legends of it down and down and down through the eons, across all those thousands of years of darkness that followed the time of destruction. That great lost city, that barely remembered paradise, that vanished realm of miracles and wonders—what tales they must have told of it! And went on telling, year after year, century after century, while the ice slowly retreated, and mankind rediscovered the skills of farming, and learned to build towns and villages, and eventually, in Sumer and Egypt and China, began once more to approach the level of accomplishment that we call "civilization."

The astounding thing, the utterly unbelievable thing, is this: that the old legends didn't even begin to tell the full story of how miraculous Atlantis really was. The actual Atlantis of the year 18,862 B.C., with its steamships and its electricity and its astonishing architectural and engineering marvels, is tremendously more fantastic than any of the Greek or Roman talespinners ever imagined.

I mean it. So far as technology goes, it's right up there with today's New York or Paris or London in many ways, only much more beautiful than any of them. And it existed all the way back here in Stone Age times, when no one else in the rest of the world had managed to get very far beyond living in caves and fashioning knives and axes out of pieces of flint.

Right now I have no explanation of how this could have been possible. None whatever.

Prince Ramifon Sigiliterimor's return to the isle of Atlantis involved him in so much ritual and formality that I began to think I was never going to get to see the city at all. We remained cooped up on the ship for an incredible length of time. It was almost as crazy-making as those days of waiting around at Thibarak harbor for the end of the departure rituals so that the royal fleet could finally set out.

First came the Ritual of Homecoming. In this one the Prince gave thanks for his safe voyage home with a lot of praying and burning of incense and the sacrifice of a bull. The Prince performed the sacrifice with his own hands. I hated having to watch at such close range, but I didn't have any choice. At least he killed the animal fast. He's evidently had a lot of practice. He used a jewel-hilted blade made of what almost certainly was *steel*. I find that fascinating in a creepy sort of way, don't you? That they'd use high-technology stuff like a steel weapon to perform a barbaric rite like animal sacrifice, I mean. A weird mix. The bull was actually an aurochs, that extinct ancestor of modern cattle, an enormous beast with terrifying black-tipped curving horns at least a yard long.

I thought we'd be going ashore then, but no, after a lot of chanting and parading around, and a feast of charred, half-raw aurochs meat that made me glad the Prince was putting it in his digestive tract and not in mine—though it's sometimes hard to tell the difference when you're a time-trip passenger, you know—the Prince went belowdecks and busied himself in front of a little shrine in the captain's cabin, invoking this god and that, for hours. A team of priests came on board and took part in this;

but when they left, Prince Ram remained on the ship.

Night fell. Crowds stood along the quay, singing and hailing the Prince. He waved back at them from the deck of his flagship. There was a fireworks display such as I've never seen in my life.

In the morning, the Prince's younger brother and sister came to give him the official family welcome. Princess Rayna is about fifteen, I'd say, and Prince Caiminor maybe thirteen. They look very much like Prince Ram, stocky and short, olive-hued skin, dark eyebrows.

Their reunion with their brother was all very formal, with touching of fingertips taking the place of kissing. The Ritual of Greeting lasted right on into mid-afternoon. Then at last they escorted him from the ship, and—by courtesy of my carrier, Prince Ramifon Sigiliterimor Septagimot Stolifax Blayl, Premianor Tisilan of Athilan, I got a chance finally to set foot on the shore of lost Atlantis.

But I didn't get very far. Off we went to the nearby Temple of the Dolphins, where a kind of tent had been set up for the Prince just inside the outermost row of perfect marble columns. Here he had to be purified, purged of any taint that he might have picked up while dwelling among the grubby uncivilized people of the mainland.

This Rite of Purification took *another* day and a night. They bathed him in milk and covered him with the petals of red and yellow flowers and chanted again and again, "May you be free of all uncleanness. May you be free of all uncleanness." On and on and on. "May the dirt of the mainland no longer cling to your skin," they chanted. "May you be free of all uncleanness." Over and over, until I thought I'd lose my mind.

But it taught me something important about this place. There's real four-star racism here. That's what the Rite of Purification is all about. The Athilantans have deep contempt for the mainlanders. *They* are the dirt of the mainland from which the rite is supposed to cleanse the Prince.

The Athilantan name for the mainlanders is "the dirt people."

My command of Athilantan grammar isn't yet as strong as I'd like it to be, so I'm not sure whether they mean that the mainlanders *live* in dirt (that is, their scruffy caves and lean-tos) or that they actually *are* dirt. But I think it's the latter.

So these noble, splendid, magnificently civilized Athilantans regard the people of Stone Age Europe as not much more than animals. Have you noticed that, too, out in Naz Glesim? Maybe it's different there, where just a handful of Athilantans live in the midst of hundreds of mainlanders. They'd have to be more careful there. But here, where there isn't a mainland face to be seen, the Athilantans don't even try to hide their scorn for them.

"We thank you, O Gods, for the return of our beloved Prince to the human realm from the land of the dirt people."

Get that little distinction, Lora. The Prince has returned to the *human* realm.

I suppose we can't really blame the Athilantans

for feeling superior, considering that they live in amazing marble palaces with electric lighting and indoor plumbing while the rest of the world lives in crude Stone Age ways. Still, it's going too far, I think, to insist that the Stone Age people on the mainland aren't even human. Backward, yes, by Athilantan standards. But to say that they aren't human? That's sheer arrogance.

When you take into account how deeply the Athilantans seem to despise the mainlanders, my earlier notion about why there haven't been any Athilantan artifacts found in any of the Paleolithic sites our archaeologists have excavated makes even more sense. If you've been ruled for thousands of years by a superior race that regards you as dirt, and suddenly the homeland of that superior race gets blown to kingdom come by a volcano, that gives you a good opportunity to rise up and kill all the surviving overlords. And then you might just want to take every last scrap of material belonging to your former masters that reminds you of your subjugation —every jar and dish and sculpture and even their tools, useful though they might be—and dump it all in the ocean while you're at it. Makes sense to me.

We need to check it out via time-search. Once we've begun our studies of the actual destruction epoch of Athilantan history, we ought to try to find out what happened afterward on the mainland, whether there really was the kind of purge of the hated masters that I'm suggesting. I think it stands to reason that there was, considering the ugly racist attitudes I've started to uncover in the Athilantan culture.

Anyway: I ought to go on with my story. I'm here to observe, not to judge.

The Ritual of Purification came to a glorious finale, with Prince Ram clambering into an alabaster tub filled with wine and honey and coming forth dripping wet while choirs of priests and priestesses sang hosannas. Servants robed him in a kind of toga of fine-spun white cotton trimmed with blue, which is what everyone wears here. (The white-and-blue color scheme, like the marble buildings with the fine stone columns, helps to reinforce the general Greek atmosphere of Athilan. As does the sunny springlike climate.) And off he went, with me watching goggle-eyed from my vantage point within his mind, down the whole tremendous length of the Concourse of the Sky *on foot* to pay his formal respects to his mighty father, Harinamur, Grand Darionis of Athilan.

The procession took all day. The Concourse of the Sky is lined on both sides by splendid majestic buildings of classical design—it's as grand a street as the Champs Elysees, or Fifth Avenue, or Piccadilly— and people looked down from every window as the Prince went by. He was bareheaded and wore nothing but that toga and sandals. The sun was very strong as he set out, but by midday the sky darkened and the usual daily rain came, a terrific downpour. He didn't seem even to notice. I don't know how long a walk it was—miles—but he never gave a hint that he might be getting tired.

And eventually he reached the imperial palace,

a splendid many-columned marble building that sits high up on a huge stone platform overlooking a great plaza, at the far end of the Concourse of the Stars.

He paused there, at the foot of a flight of what must have been at least a hundred immense marble steps, and looked up and up and up. At the top of this colossal stone staircase was a broad porch. His father the King was waiting there for him. And Prince Ram, who had just walked something like ten or eleven hours through the streets of the city to reach this place without resting even for a moment, unhesitatingly began to climb those hundred gigantic steps.

"Hail, O One King," the Prince cried. "Harinamur, Grand Darionis! And then—in a softer voice: "Father."

"Ram," the king said. And they embraced.

It was incredibly touching. Mighty father, invincible son: so happy to see each other again, so intensely happy. I was always fairly close with my own father, you know. But I never felt, with him, anything remotely like the powerful force of love that was passing between these two as they hugged, in full view of the Athilantan multitudes, on that gleaming marble porch atop those hundred giant stairs.

It was a little embarrassing, too, eavesdropping on Prince Ram's feelings in this moment of reunion. But you have to force yourself not to think about things like that. As I've said before, and hardly need to point out to you, being a time-traveler involves being a sneak and a snooper and an eavesdropper on somebody else's most private moments, and there's simply no way around it. Since we can't go to the past ourselves, we have to invade the minds of its inhabitants without their knowing it, and you can't pretend that there's anything very nice about that. But it's necessary. That's the only justification there is. If we're going to salvage anything out of the vanished past, we have to do it this way, because this is the only way there is.

The King is the most awesome human being I have ever seen. In grandeur and presence and authority he is like a combination of Moses, Abraham Lincoln, and the Emperor Augustus. He's very tall, particularly for an Athilantan, with long white hair and a thick, full, white beard. He has a look of such nobility and wisdom that you want to drop down before him and kiss his sandals. This day he was dressed in purple robes woven through with thread of gold and silver, and he wore a crown made of laurel leaves set on golden spikes.

With immense solemnity he took Prince Ram in his arms and held him close, and then he stepped back so that they could look in each other's eyes; and in the King's dark shining eyes I saw such warmth, such depths of love, that I actually felt sad and envious, thinking that no one else on Earth could ever have been loved by his father the way this prince was.

"We have missed you every day of your absence, and every hour of every day," the King said. "We have asked the gods daily to preserve you and bring you safely back to us. And now our prayers have been answered."

"Father. Grand Darionis. One King. My thoughts have ever been upon you while I traveled abroad."

They touched fingertips, very quickly and delicately, in the formal Athilantan manner.

Then six priests appeared, leading out another aurochs, and father and son slaughtered the poor beast right then and there, each of them wielding one of those jewel-hilted swords. A fire was lit; the meat was cooked; the priests hacked chunks off the carcass and brought them to the King and the Prince, who fed each other with their own hands.

It was, I know, meant as a ceremony of renewed love. But to me it also seemed a bloody, barbaric business, and I was glad when it ended and the Prince and his father went side by side into the royal palace.

You would not easily believe the splendor of the place. The lavish draperies, the carvings in ivory and jade, the many-colored stone pillars and filigreed window openings—it's your basic *Arabian Nights* palace made real. You look at it and your heart aches, because you can't help telling yourself that all of it is doomed to wind up at the bottom of the Atlantic Ocean, buried under thousands of years of muck and silt. You stand amid all this fantastic dreamlike loveliness and you know that its days are numbered, that it's not going to last beyond next month, or next year, or maybe next century at best, and it *hurts* to think about it. (The ruins of the palace must still be down there on the ocean floor somewhere! But could we ever find them? And would any shred of their beauty still remain?)

Each member of the royal family has a private suite of rooms within the palace. Prince Ram's suite is in back, on the second floor, looking out over a courtyard and garden. It's grand enough to make any king happy. I wonder what the King's own rooms are like, if this is what a prince gets.

By this time Ram was so groggy with fatigue that I was having trouble making sense of his thoughts. Everything that was passing through his mind was reaching me in blurred and woolly form. He tried to pretend that he was fine, and for a time he and the King sat together in one of Ram's rooms, discussing some important governmental matters that I couldn't follow at all.

But it was obvious to the King that Ram wasn't able to keep his eyes open, and after a little while he bade his son goodnight and left. The Prince ran through the usual set of end-of-day prayers in one almighty hurry and dropped down on his bed like a dead man.

I let him rest for half the night. But there was too much that I wanted to tell you. So I took control of him and we went looking for writing materials, and found them, and for the last two hours I've had him setting all this down on long strips of vellum. His mind is still asleep, so he's getting the rest he needs. But he's going to have an awfully sore hand tomorrow from this much scribbling. I think I'd better stop now, though. It's close to dawn. Out where you are, thousands of miles to the east, the sun is already up. I hope you're okay. And that you get a chance to see this fantastic place for yourself some day.

Signing off—

—Roy

□ FIVE □

DAY 36, NEW LIGHT, GREAT RIVER.

One more letter, sent off into the unknown. Will it reach you? Will you ever write back to me? Who knows?

I might as well admit it: I haven't really been doing too well lately. Now and then I get spells when I begin to feel lost and gloomy here, cut off, out of contact with anything real. All too aware that what I am is a floating ghost implanted in another man's body while my own lies sleeping in a laboratory at the other end of time.

And then I remind myself of what a privilege it is to be here—to have been allowed to conduct part of this amazing exploration of times lost and, so we all once believed, forever irrecoverable. To be experiencing the sights and sounds and wonders of this incredible era, an era of whose very existence we once had only the most pathetic distorted notions.

How remarkable that is—how much I am to be envied—!

I suppose I don't really need to be saying things like this to you. You're in the same boat I am. Forgive me for being dull or obvious. These matters weigh on my mind.

Sometimes I wish we'd never volunteered for any of this, Lora, that we were back in our own real time right this minute, you and I walking hand in hand in the park, or running along the beach, or just sitting quietly together having a pizza. Ordinary trivial things that everybody takes for granted. Home Era is starting to seem unreal to me. I have to stop and remind myself what an ice cream sundae tastes like, or what kind of sound a guitar makes, or even—God help me—what color your eyes are. And then everything starts to cut pretty close.

Well, the moods come and go. They can't be helped.

But I know we'll get home eventually, if everything goes right. There'll be plenty of time for pizza and ice cream then, and all the rest. Meanwhile the basic thing to remember is that we're in the middle of the most fantastic adventure anybody could imagine. There you are in Stone Age Europe with mammoths walking around on the tundra—and here I am waking up every morning to the golden sunlight of fabulous Atlantis—

How could anybody dare to feel gloomy even for a moment, doing what we're doing? The idea's practically obscene.

*　　*　　*

Busy days here. Lots of new information.

This is what I've learned about the Athilantan system of government in the past few days:

The King is an absolute monarch, and I mean *absolute*. Whatever he says, goes. There's no council of nobles, no senate, nothing that remotely challenges the King's authority. He's got courtiers and bureaucrats, sure, but the whole empire is essentially his own private property, to rule as he pleases.

It sounds like a recipe for disaster. Certainly such an arrangement always has been, in historical times. No empire can hope to have an unbroken string of capable rulers. This king or that one might be all right, and maybe as much as a century can go along without any troublemakers reaching the throne. But sooner or later some madman is bound to come along, a Nero or a Caligula or a Hitler, somebody who won't be able to handle absolute power, who runs amok and causes terrible chaos.

Why hasn't it happened here? How has the Athilantan empire managed to survive for so many hundreds of years without producing a power-crazed tyrant who brings everything crashing down?

The clue, it seems, is in the title that they give the King. Grand Darionis literally means The One King, and by that they mean that *he is the only king that Athilan has ever had*. The present ruler is considered to be the reincarnation of everyone who has ever held the throne, all the way back to the time of the first Harinamur who founded the kingdom back in legendary times. When each king dies, all his memories pass into the soul of his successor, so that he embodies the accumulated wisdom of the entire dynasty. Or so they say. I don't yet know if that's literally true, or just a picturesque way of asserting the strength of tradition here. I can tell you that the look in King Harinamur's eyes is not a look I have ever seen in anyone else's. He seems almost superhuman.

I think this One King business is at least in part responsible for the unusual degree of closeness that exists between the King and Prince Ram.

After all, Ram is the heir to the throne. If I understand these things correctly, when it is his time to become Grand Darionis he will in effect *become identical with his father.* The King may already regard Ram as nothing more than a literal continuation of his own identity. And Ram may already have come to see himself as the actual reincarnation of the King, the older man in a new body.

I don't really know how this works, yet. Do they have a way of transplanting the entire memory files of the King into his son? (Or daughter. As in England, the throne usually goes to the oldest child, male or female.) If so, it has to be done while the King is still alive, right? Unless they do it in the moment of death.

Or possibly, there's no literal transfer of memory at all, and the whole concept is just a kind of convention, a political fiction, like calling the Emperor of China the "Son of Heaven." If that's so, all the kings may have the same name, and they may be very closely imprinted with the beliefs and values of their predecessors, but they can't actually be regarded as identical to all the kings who have gone before them.

So far, I've probed Ram very cautiously about this whole matter. It may be a really sensitive area for him, in which case he might become aware of me as I go poking around in his mind. That's the last thing I need.

What I've learned, though, seems to indicate that they really do have some way of merging minds, personalities, stored memories, and such. And it's done in stages, each one marked with a big ceremony.

First comes the Rite of Designation, in which the young child is named as heir apparent. This is done at the age of ten.

Then there's the Rite of Joining, at thirteen. I don't quite understand what this is, but it involves creating some kind of deep bond between the ruler and his heir. My guess is that it's the opening of a sort of mental conduit through which psychic impulses flow from the older one to the younger—the beginning of the transfer.

The third step is the Rite of Anointing. That happens when the heir apparent is eighteen, which means the Anointing of Ram ought to be due to take place very soon now. In this, the Prince enters full adulthood and heavy responsibility. He receives certain mystic powers, which are so secret that not even Ram himself seems to know what they are yet. He gets to live in a palace of his own. And he becomes a kind of viceroy of the realm, a junior king, with areas of authority and obligation far beyond anything he's had to undertake before. Once this rite is performed, he is permitted to marry. Is *expected* to marry, as a matter of fact.

(As far as I can tell, Prince Ram, with the Rite of Anointing just around the corner, has no particular woman in mind to become his Princess. Perhaps she'll be chosen for him by his father and her identity won't be made known to him until the official moment. Brrr!)

The fourth and final rite is the Rite of Union. This, I assume, is the ultimate transfer of identity from king to prince, as the time gets close for the handing over of the throne to the chosen heir. When this takes place, or how, I don't know. All details concerning this rite are buried so deeply in Prince Ram's consciousness that I'd need to do major excavation to get to them. Obviously it's something he doesn't want to think about, or isn't allowed to.

What will it be like for me, I wonder, when Prince Ram experiences the Rite of Union? What will it feel like when all those additional mental impulses come flooding into his mind? Pretty chaotic, I imagine. I suspect it'll be something like sitting up in the top of a tall tree while a hurricane is going on all around you.

But of course I might not even be here by the time he does the Rite of Union. We've only got a six-month assignment here, after all. As I say, I have no way of telling how soon Ram is due for the fourth rite, but my guess is that it's going to be more than six months down the line.

Some real mixed feelings here. On the one hand I'm uneasy about the impact of the Rite of Union on me if I'm still inside Ram's mind when it happens. On the other hand I suddenly realize that I'm hoping Home Era will let me stick around long enough to observe it, regardless of the dangers. The rite would probably give me answers to a lot of the questions I'm starting to ask myself about Athilan. I don't want to be yanked back to our own time until I'm good and ready to go. Until I've soaked up everything I can possibly learn about this place.

But of course I've got no control over that. When the time's up, back to Home Era I go, whether or not I want to. I return to "reality." I return to *you*. But I give up Atlantis. Don't misunderstand me, Lora. I'd give anything to be with you again after this separation. And yet, and yet—to be here for the Rite of Union—to have a ringside seat when all the accumulated memories of all the kings of Athilan go pouring into Prince Ram's mind—

Well, we'll see. It's entirely out of my hands. I don't care for that very much. There are times when I feel like a puppet on a string. Which I know is a dumb attitude. It was understood from the start that we were here only for a specific length of time and then we'd be brought back to Home Era. That was the deal, and no use complaining about it now. All the same, I have a funny feeling that I'm going to resent it when they yank me back, because it's going to come just as something tremendously important is about to happen.

Why am I worrying so much? All this fidgeting and dithering about things?

Just lonely, I guess. Thinking of you. Missing

you. Maybe sending "emotionally connected pairs" on these trips into the past isn't such a great idea after all.

The Prince is an active and vigorous young man, and his days are full ones.

He's up at dawn. Prayers, first. (These Athilantans are very devout. They seem to have a couple of dozen gods, who are, however, all regarded as aspects of the One God.) Then, before breakfast, he swims in the marble-lined pool in the courtyard of the palace's rear wing. Fifty laps. (Everything here seems to be made out of marble. There's a big stonequarry somewhere on the far side of Mount Balamoris, but also they bring finer grades of marble in by ship from Greece and Italy.)

Breakfast, then. Fruits, most of them strange tropical ones that I can't identify, followed by roast lamb. And a rich, sweet red wine. Wine for breakfast— well, that isn't anything I'd care to do. But the Prince is strong as an ox and it doesn't even make him a little bit tipsy. And these Athilantans, like all the Mediterranean peoples who I believe are descended from them, love their wine. There are vineyards all over the island. (All their wines are sweet. I know that real wine connoisseurs claim that the best wines are dry ones, but the Athilantans probably wouldn't care. They like it the way they like it. I suppose a Frenchman wouldn't approve, if there were any Frenchmen in existence. But there aren't any yet. Nor are there any vineyards right now, over there in the icebound land that will someday be France.

And there aren't going to be for thousands of years.)

After breakfast Ram meets with the King. They go over all sorts of official documents and reports.

Most of what they deal with concerns the flow of raw materials that Athilantan ships bring in from Africa and southern Europe. These Athilantans are the world's first imperialists. They've colonized every part of the world within reach, importing things they need—minerals, mostly, but certain foodstuffs also—and giving not very much in return. Of course there isn't much that they *could* give, considering how primitive all the other humans of this era are. Your typical modern-era colonial power imports raw materials from backward countries and exports manufactured goods, but semi-nomadic Stone Age hunters don't have a lot of need for light bulbs, fancy plumbing fixtures, or rubber tires.

There's a *tremendous* cultural gulf between the Athilantans and the rest of the Stone Age world. It's incredible. They are so far beyond everybody else here in all ways that I can't even begin to explain it. A mutant race of supergeniuses that mysteriously arose out of nowhere during the late Paleolithic Era? That sounds too hokey to be believed. But what other explanation can there be?

The King and the Prince also discuss local matters at their morning conference. They decide which government officials deserve promotions and which need to be reprimanded for slacking off. They talk about street repair and new building construction. They make plans for upcoming religious festivals.

None of this is very romantic. It's just their job—
ruling the Athilantan Empire. And it's a lot of work,
which never eases off.

Lunch is light: some grapes, some cheese, and
the strange bread, hard as rock, that they make out
of the wheat that grows here. Wheat is still in its
early evolutionary stages and such wheat as they
have isn't very different from grass seed. But even
that is amazing, considering how far in the past we
are. Still, it doesn't make remarkably good bread.
The Prince drinks a light white wine with lunch, as
sweet as perfume. Ugh.

Then a nap. And then he goes off for afternoon
exercise: horseback riding, javelin throwing, another
swim, and the like. He's a terrific athlete. You'd
have to be, to ride the horses they have in this
era—mean little guys, short legs, long manes, angry
dispositions. They're wild animals and they don't
pretend otherwise. The Athilantans understand the
principle of the saddle but they don't know anything
about bridles and bits, and their technique for controlling their horses is basically to grab them around
the necks and wrestle them into submission.

After exercise, there's usually some ritual to perform. This is a very religious country, in its way.
The place swarms with priests and priestesses of the
various gods. All these gods constantly demand wor-
ship. The various rituals invariably involve the King
and the Prince, because the King of Athilan is not
only the monarch but also the high priest, and the
Prince is his right-hand man. So they have to put in
an hour or so in this temple or that one almost every

day, presiding over these godly matters. The chants and prayers they utter are highly stylized and I don't have a clear idea of what they mean. A lot of animal sacrifice goes on, too. I still don't find that very easy to take.

In late afternoon the whole royal family gets together for a kind of relaxation hour, warm and affectionate, everybody funny and loving. Then they have dinner together, a terrific feast. The servants are mainlanders. (Slaves, I suppose. I have to keep reminding myself not to expect the Athilantans to abide by all our nice modern democratic institutions, like freedom. Like the Romans, like the Greeks, like a lot of advanced civilizations of antiquity, the Athilantans don't seem to see anything wrong with enslaving people. It's always a surprise, isn't it, when people who seem generally enlightened, like the Athilantans, turn out to practice something as cruel and wrong as slavery. But the past is the past, and things are different there, and no use expecting it to be otherwise. At least they seem to treat their slaves pretty well, for what that's worth.)

There's food galore at these royal feasts, a simply incredible amount of food, usually with a roasted ox as the main event, and amazing quantities of wine. (But everybody seems to stay sober. Is the wine very weak, or do these people have unusual tolerance for alcohol?)

Minstrels come in and sing when dinner is over. The favorite is a long historical epic, something like the *Iliad* and the *Odyssey* rolled into one. It sounds very stirring, but it also happens to be snug in some ancient version of the Athilantan language, and it's as hard for Prince Ram to understand as Chaucer's English would be for us. I can get only the vaguest drift of it, something about exile and wandering and the eventual building of this great city on the island of Athilan.

Listening to the minstrels gives me a wonderful feeling of what it must have been like to sit around the banquet hall in ancient Greece, listening to Homer strumming on his lyre and chanting the first editions of his poems. But then I have to tell myself that Greece isn't ancient yet—that it won't even exist as a concept for another 17,000 years and some—and that Homer, Achilles, Agamemnon, and the rest of that legendary crowd are unknown figures of the unimaginably misty future, so far as the Athilantans are concerned.

It gets dark early here. The Prince goes to sleep when the minstrels are finished, and sleeps like a marble statue until the first rays of dawn.

Or, at least, *would* sleep like a marble statue if I didn't insist on hauling him out of bed somewhere during the night so that he could write the letters for me. Of course he's completely unaware of that. I keep the letters hidden in a leather case underneath a stack of old togas that he doesn't seem to wear any more. Whenever I hear that a courier is about to set out for Naz Glesim, I put the Prince into trance and have him get the current letter and pack it up for shipment. I wonder, of course, if any of my letters will ever get to you. The distances are so great, the situation so tricky. But I have to keep on writing them. I need this contact with you so very much— even one-sided as it's been up till now.

I wish I had some way of dictating my impressions of this world into a recorder that I could take back to Home Era with me. The big trouble with being a disembodied web of electrical impulses, I keep thinking, is that you can't carry anything across time with you except the contents of your own mind. Better than nothing, but pretty frustrating all the same. I'd like to come home with bulging notebooks describing everything I've seen here, and maybe a suitcase or two of Athilantan artifacts. No way, though. No way at all.

Time to go. Ram's writing hand is cramping badly. He needs to rest. And, I think, so do I.

—Roy

□ S I X □

DAY 5, MONTH OF WESTERN WIND, Year of Great River.

Almost a week since my last letter. I haven't wanted to write. Strange things have been going on in my mind and I didn't particularly care to talk about them, hoping they'd vanish of their own accord. But they haven't.

What's happening—not to be mysterious about it any longer—is that I've been feeling a powerful urge to let Prince Ram know I'm here.

I realize that this is a classic malady of time-travelers. The compulsion to stand up and shout, "Look at me! Look at me! I'm sitting right here inside your head!" There's even a name for it, isn't there? Observer Guilt Syndrome, I think. But knowing that I'm not the first one to experience this doesn't make it any easier for me.

The thing is that I have now spent several weeks observing Prince Ram at the closest possible range. I feel closer to him than any friend or wife could ever be. I know which side of his mouth he prefers to chew his food on, which god's name he takes in vain when he stubs his toe, and the details of the really nasty trick he pulled on his kid brother when he was nine years old. (And which he still feels guilty about, although Prince Caiminor was only four at the time and probably doesn't remember a thing.)

All this is producing the predictable Observer Guilt reactions in me. Maybe you're feeling a little of it yourself. I talked about this a few letters back— when I compared being an observer to being a spy, and said that it felt a little ugly. But it's starting to seem like something a lot worse than spying, now. It feels like being a Peeping Tom. A spy, at least, is serving his country. Peeping Toms are simply slimy.

I know, Lora, I know, I know. I'm serving the cause of knowledge by doing what I'm doing. And my training is supposed to help me get past these expectable feelings of guilt and shame.

But the longer I stay in Prince Ram's mind, the better I get to know him and the more I admire him. He is a strong, capable, intelligent, determined, disciplined, *princely* fellow. He has his flaws—who doesn't?—but he's basically a very good person who is going to be a great king some day. And the more I get to like him, the less I like myself for skulking here, invisible and imperceptible, inside his head. I'm coming to hate the sneakiness of it: eavesdropping on his conversations and even his most private thoughts, and putting him into trances that he doesn't in any way suspect so that I can use him to write these letters for me.

I want to let him know that I'm here—a visitor from the remote future who has come to study the great and glorious Athilantan empire in its heyday. I want to ask his permission, I guess, for continuing to occupy my hidden perch within his mind.

Don't worry. I haven't given him even the slightest hint so far. But in the past week I've come close, a couple of times, to making actual conscious-level contact with him. And the temptation isn't going away. If anything, it's getting stronger.

For the time being, I'm being very cautious about the degree of mind-entry I'm allowing myself with the Prince. Mostly I limit myself to low-level passive observation, simply monitoring minute-by-minute sensory information: what he sees, what he hears, and so forth.

I'm not trying to do any digging into the deeper stored data of his mind. That's the easiest way, of course, to make your host suspicious that something peculiar is going on in his head. And what I'm afraid of is that if he expresses any sort of suspicion that he has been possessed or inhabited or somehow taken over by an alien spirit, I'm going to blurt out the whole truth to him in a wild rush of confessional zeal. I don't dare risk that.

This is creating some serious disadvantages for me.

For example, without taking a deeper look into his mind, I have no way of understanding the significance of the unusual and apparently very important ritual that the Prince and his father performed last night.

In late afternoon a messenger came to the Prince and said, "It is the night of Romany Star."

I'm sure that's what he said: *Romany Star.*

The Prince, who had been relaxing after a strenuous workout on horseback, immediately called for his slaves, who bathed him, sprinkled him with some kind of aromatic oil, and clothed him in a shining scarlet robe (which looked very much like silk. Is the silkworm native to Athilan, or do their ships travel as far as China?) and a little silver coronet. Then he went to the uppermost floor of the palace, where there is a staircase leading to a roof-top garden.

King Harinamur was waiting for him up there in the garden, wearing a silken robe even showier than the Prince's, and a beautifully worked golden coronet. There was nobody else present, no priests, no slaves.

Darkness began to fall. Father and son, working quickly, took long slender twigs and branches of some delicately colored aromatic wood from a storage chest against the wall, and arranged them on a little altar of green stone (jade?). Then they waited, standing stock still, staring rigidly at the sky. They were both looking at the same sector, almost directly overhead. I could feel Prince Ram slipping into a kind of trance of his own accord. His pulse rate rose, his eyes were dilated, his skin temperature dropped.

The stars were appearing, now. The unfamiliar constellations of the Paleolithic sky blazed above us.

Ram's head was thrown back, his eyes were fixed.
He scarcely even blinked.

"I see it," he said after a time, in a strange
throaty voice, like a man talking in his sleep.

"Do you, so soon?" said the King. "Yes, young
eyes would."

"Above the Great Whale. To the left of the
Spear."

"Yes. Yes. I see it too. Hail, Romany Star!"

"Hail," murmured the Prince. "Romany Star!"

And then they began to chant, slowly, solemnly,
in the ancient priestly language.

I was too awed—frightened, even—to try to pen-
etrate Ram's mind and seek the meaning. They were
like two statues, motionless but for their lips, staring
up at that star and uttering their prayer to it. I think
I know which star they were looking at: a brilliant
one, a giant. It seemed to be of a reddish color. I'm
no astronomer and I couldn't even begin to guess
which star it was, and in any case the sky over
Athilan is nothing like the sky we see back in Home
Era.

Ram dropped deeper and deeper into trance.
He seemed scarcely conscious now, and his father
the same. The prayer went on and on, slow, som-
ber, profoundly moving even though I couldn't comprehend a syllable of it. It was like some long, intricate
poem. No: it was more like a prayer for the dead.
Tears were quietly rolling down Ram's cheeks as he
spoke.

Now they knelt and lit the twigs they had placed
on the stone altar, and curling wisps of fragrant

smoke rose above them. Calmly Ram began to rip his splendid silken gown to shreds; and calmly the King did likewise. They tore those gowns to ribbons, and cast the ribbons into the flame, so that they stood naked by the altar, wearing nothing but their coronets of gold and silver. And then they removed the coronets too, and crushed them in their bare hands, and tossed them on the fire.

The rite, whatever it was, was over.

Naked, still entranced, the King and the Prince turned and slowly made their way back into the palace. No one dared look at them. They parted, without a word, in the grand hallway, each going to his own suite. Ram went to his bedroom, lay down without bothering with the usual evening prayers, and fell instantly asleep. And that was the rite of Romany Star.

I don't have any idea what it was all about. But it was obviously more important than any of the other religious rites the Prince has taken part in since I've been here. He treated all the other ones simply as mere tasks, part of the job of being a prince. This one moved him deeply. This one shook him to his depths. I need to know why. If I were in better shape myself, I'd scout around in his mind until I found out. But right now I don't dare make any sort of contact with him at that level. I simply don't dare.

—Roy

□ S E V E N □

DAY 11, WESTERN WIND, GREAT RIVER.

A big day for me.

The first letter from you in Naz Glesim came in today, with the regular diplomatic packet! I must have read it a dozen times. It was such an incredible joy, hearing from you after all this time, these weeks and weeks of being cooped up by myself inside Prince Ram's mind.

I have to confess it now; I was getting a little paranoid about not hearing from you. I know, I know, it takes forever for couriers to get from one end of the empire to the other. So I couldn't really have expected an answer from you any sooner than this. But here I was, sending off pages and pages of stuff to you and never getting even a postcard back, so to speak, and the time was passing—passing *very* slowly, let me tell you—and it seemed like years had gone by. I wondered if you were too busy to write. Or just didn't want to bother. And various other unworthy thoughts. It also occurred to me that something terrible might have happened to you. The time-travel process isn't absolutely safe, after all.

I kept all these worries to myself when writing to you. Or tried to, at least. But now none of it matters, because I know that you're all right, that you still care, that you've been answering my letters as soon as you could. And so on and so forth. And how glad I am!

The officials who sort through the stuff that Provincial Governor Sippurilayl sends to the capital from Naz Glesim must have been very puzzled indeed to unroll a scroll addressed to Prince Ram and discover that the whole thing was in some unknown kind of writing. But they came to the only logical conclusion—that it must be written in code, and therefore very important—and they brought it to the Prince right away.

Now came the ticklish part. The Prince glanced at it and thought it was all just some crazy scribble, and to my absolute horror he started to toss it in the fire. I had to override him and pull him back to his desk, *right in front of the officials who had brought him the scroll.* He stopped short, struggled against my override for a second, almost fell down.

God knows what they thought was happening to him—another "stroke," maybe. Ram didn't understand it either. But he waved them quickly out of his office, perhaps because he was embarrassed at having them see him staggering around like that and was afraid it might happen again in another minute.

The instant they were out of the room, I put

him in trance and read your letter. And re-read it and re-read it, hungrily. It was so wonderful hearing from you at last that I came close to breaking into tears. (With Prince Ram's eyes!) Then when I knew your letter practically by heart I had the Prince roll it up and hide it away in the alcove where I keep letters waiting to go to you, and I awakened him, after trying to wipe from his memory all recollection of what had been taking place.

If I'm lucky, he won't recall a thing about the strange scroll with the peculiar writing on it. More likely he'll be left with some vague, misty impression of having been looking at a document that made no sense to him. My hope is that the Prince will think that he dreamed the whole thing—the way someone can dream of picking up a book in Greek or Arabic and is able, in his sleep, at least, to read it with complete understanding, even though he can't remember a word of it afterward.

At any rate, you sound happy and healthy and generally in great shape, and I'm glad for you. I'm relieved to hear that the weather isn't as awful as I feared. Cold, yes, but that's only to be expected in Ice Age Europe, and at least it hasn't been snowing much. The description you give of the house where you're living, made entirely of mammoth bones, is fascinating. The foundation of mammoth skulls, the wall of mammoth jawbones stacked crosswise like that, the huge thighbones forming an entranceway—I guess that's what passes for a grand mansion out Naz Glesim way. Naturally the Athilantan Provincial Governor would have the best accommodations, such as they are.

Very interesting about that ugly, shaggy-looking character with the receding chin and the sloping forehead who was seen skulking around outside the village. Do you think there's really any likelihood that he's a Neanderthal? My understanding of these things is that the Neanderthals have been extinct for a long time now, fifteen or twenty thousand years, at least. But I guess it's possible that a few of them still linger on in the back woods, drifting around like sad displaced outcasts.

(We keep finding out, don't we, how little we actually knew about prehistoric man in the days before time exploration began! Of course all we had to go by was a little scattering of skeletons that had survived by flukes here and there, and an assortment of stone tools and weapons. And out of that we conjured up some kind of notion of hundreds of thousands of years of human life. It was a pretty good guess, I suppose, considering the data we had. But now that we're actually back here seeing it for ourselves, how different it all looks. Neanderthal Man isn't completely gone after all, if your idea is correct. And the Paleolithic *Homo sapiens* people have a much more elaborate culture than we ever imagined. And then, of course, there are these spectacular Athilantan folk, whose existence we never even remotely suspected, dominating everything, operating a modern technological civilization all the way back here. With *electricity*, no less.)

Now that I know you are in fact getting my letters, and are able to write back, I'll probably write more often. And I hope you will too. It was magical the way hearing from you dissolved the terrible sense of isolation I've been feeling, the miserable loneliness, the fidgety worrying about problems that didn't really need to be worried about. I can hardly wait for the next one from you.

Of course it's risky, isn't it? Not only because we have to take control of our host's body to write our letters, but because having all these bizarre scrolls in an unknown language traveling back and forth is eventually likely to make someone suspect sorcery, or espionage, or something else serious. There could be an investigation, I suppose. But it's worth it, despite the risks, don't you think? I'm absolutely convinced of that. Getting that letter from you this morning was one of the great moments of my life. To find out that you're okay, to hear about what you've been doing these past weeks, to read those words, "I love you." Now I want the next letter. And the next. And the one after that.

Got to stop now. More later.

And now it *is* later—a little before dawn.

Big trouble. The Prince knows I'm here.

Although I haven't been monitoring his mind deeply for some time now, for reasons which you already know, I can't help but be aware of the mental vibrations he gives off. When he's excited, I feel it. When he's angry. When he's tired. When he's tense. It's a constant broadcast that I automatically pick up.

Today, a couple of hours after the episode of the arrival of your letter and my overriding of his attempt to throw it on the fire, I began detecting a new and troublesome mood in him. It was somewhere between anxiety and anger, and it was growing stronger moment by moment, a slow, steady buildup of tension that had to be leading to some sort of explosion.

That was pretty scary, feeling him ticking away like a bomb. I was tempted to reach in and try to defuse him before he went off. But I didn't know where to reach or what to defuse. So I waited uneasily, wondering what was going to happen, while he went on working himself up.

Then at last he spoke—mentally, loud and clear—directly to me. It was like a bomb going off right in my face:

—*Who are you, demon, and why are you within me?*

Remember when I said that what we really are is demons, taking possession of the minds and bodies of our hosts? That's the way Prince Ram sees it too.

I was totally stunned. I didn't know what to say or do or think.

This was my chance, if ever there was one, to make direct contact with the Prince. As you know if my more recent letters have been getting through to you, I've been fighting that temptation for days. Successfully. This sudden shot in the dark from the Prince might easily have broken through my will to resist Observer Guilt Syndrome. But it didn't. When the chips were down, I found myself maintaining total silence after all, just as our training tells us to do. I kept myself sealed off, allowing just minimal contact with Prince Ram's mind.

But he kept after me.

—*I know you are there. I feel you hiding in my mind.*

I remained silent. What could I do? Tell him he was imagining things? Any contact I made would have the effect of revealing me, of confirming my presence.

—*Who are you, demon? Why do you assail me?*

He was growing more excited moment by moment. He trembled and shook. His heart was pounding and there was a throbbing like a hammerblow in his temples. He knelt and covered his face with his hands. Then he pressed his hands to the sides of his head with tremendous force, as if trying to drive me out by sheer pressure. He focused all his power of concentration on the task of expelling me from his mind.

Of course none of this had any effect on me. But the strain on the Prince was fearful. Every muscle of his body was writhing. His eyes bulged, his breath came in wild gasps, sweat broke from all his pores. Stress hormones flooded his system. There was such internal violence going on all over him that it was scary. Could he harm himself like this? I didn't know.

But I had only two choices, to reveal myself or

to put him into trance and calm him down. I opted for the second choice, and he slumped and lay still.

For a time I was afraid to do anything else. Then, gradually, I began to explore the upper levels of his mind.

What I discovered was—as I suspected—that I hadn't done a complete enough job of editing out the memory of seeing your letter. He remembered just enough of it, and of the earlier letter of mine that he had seen that time when his steward had walked in on him aboard the ship. That led him to think about the odd stumble he had taken that afternoon, and the "stroke" he had suffered when I originally entered his mind weeks ago, and the strange sorenesses in his arm, and various other little curiosities directly related to my presence within him. And he had jumped to exactly the correct conclusion. The Prince is a highly intelligent man, you know.

I couldn't hope to cancel out all his justified suspicions by tinkering now with his mind. That would involve so much messing around that I'd certainly do great damage. I couldn't leave him conked out on the floor, either. So I settled for reaching in here and there and returning his hormonal flow to make him as calm as possible. And then I brought him out of trance.

He sat up, frowning, shaking his head. But he didn't try to communicate with me again. Simply arose, paced around the room a few times, put his head out the window, took three very deep breaths. And called his steward, and asked for a flagon of wine. Sipped a little of it. Sat staring at nothing in particular for a while, his mind almost blank. Finally said his prayers, got into bed, dropped into a deep sleep. Now it's almost morning. He hasn't awakened.

My whole mission's in danger now. I'm going to have to be extra careful about everything I do. I know he's still convinced that there's a demon in him. And he's right. The intensity of his reaction was truly frightening. I don't want him driving himself into seizures of some sort—or having a mental breakdown that could affect his position as heir to the throne. Probably I can take the risk of continuing to use him to write these letters while he's under trance, but otherwise I'll have to lay low. If worst comes to worst I may even have to abandon the whole project and return ahead of schedule to Home Era. We'll see. Keep your fingers crossed for me, love. More later, I hope.

Continued, the following day.

They have had a rite of exorcism to drive me out of the Prince's mind. Obviously, it didn't work. Even so, my position remains very precarious.

The first thing Ram did upon awakening was to summon the Counsellor Teneristis, who is a vizier of the realm and has been the Prince's special mentor for many years. Teneristis is a very short, brusque old man, businesslike and tough, with two thick tufts of wiry white hair that stick out comically from the sides of his head like horns. There's nothing in the least comic about him, though.

The Prince said, "There is a demon in me. It turns my mind dark and makes me see and do things I do not understand."

"You will go to the Labyrinth, then," Teneristis replied instantly. "You have sinned, or no demon could have entered you. And in the Labyrinth you will be purged of your sin."

The Labyrinth! Shades of Theseus and the Minotaur! But this isn't Crete and the myth of Theseus won't be invented for more thousands of years than I want to think about. The Labyrinth of Athilan isn't a prison for a monster, it's a holy sanctuary, located in a maze of dark musty caverns halfway up the flank of Mount Balamoris. My guess is that the caverns are natural ones, most likely part of the intricate geological plumbing that lies beneath most volcanos— all those tubes and vents and conduits and whatnot that a volcano creates as it rises. This volcano has been dormant for a long time and the Athilantans have honeycombed these warrens along its slopes with a network of sacred shrines.

It's a beautiful mountain. So peaceful, so lovely, that you tend to forget that one morning in the very near future it's going to come roaring back to life and destroy this whole fantastic civilization.

Alone, the Prince rode out in the early mists of morning through the white and glittering streets of Athilan, past temples and palaces, past villas and parks, up the glorious green slopes of the foothills of Mount Balamoris. And tethered his horse, and knelt, and prayed. And walked without hesitation toward the narrow mouth of the Labyrinth.

It was a bare slit, unmarked, unadorned, fairly high up the mountain. He stepped through it into an eight-sided chamber lined with white-and-blue tiles that led to a paved passageway heading inward and downward. The chamber was lit by three electrical lamps that gave off a rich golden glow. The passageway wasn't lit at all beyond the first twenty paces. Dimness engulfed him, and then even the dimness gave way to the complete absence of light. For what seemed like hours he spiraled down and down and down, far beyond the reach of the deepest beam of light, into a realm of terrifying darkness.

In that utter blackness your only guide is the sequence of smooth high-relief carvings on the walls. You grope your way, feeling for the age-old holy images, "reading" the walls with your hands. There is a logical pattern to the order of the images that makes sense to an Athilantan, though not to me, and so long as you can summon up the proper passages from the religious teachings you have studied, you'll be able to find your way. If you become confused even in the slightest detail, you get lost immediately and the chances of your being able to get out again are extremely small. So Teneristis was taking a considerable risk with the heir to the throne by sending him to the Labyrinth.

The Prince didn't seem worried. He moved along briskly, passing his hands over this carving and that one. He appeared to know what to expect as he went, and he always found it. There was only one moment—a bad one—when he paused after stroking one of the carvings and a jolt of uncertainty went through him like a spear, leaving a trail of jitter-hormones in his veins. But he halted, took a few deep breaths, forced himself to a state of icy calm, touched the carving again.

This time he found the clue that he had missed before, a double zigzag of lines to the left of the main image. Breathing more easily, he went onward.

And on and on, down and down.

The walls of the passageway were narrower here, and lower. He had to stoop and shuffle. The air grew warmer. He was wearing nothing but a loin-cloth, but even so, he became slippery with sweat. Though his mind was at ease—cool, confident—there was the awareness of danger not very far from the center of his soul. All he needed to do was take one wrong turn and he would lose himself beyond all hope. A terrible death, alone down there in the sweltering darkness, crying out for food, for water, for light.

Then I felt his heart thump with joy and he came suddenly around a sharp bend of the corridor into a place where he could actually *see*.

This was the end of the line, the core of the Labyrinth, the penitential chamber.

It was a circular room, dome-roofed, with an opening in the floor at its very center. Light came up through that opening—red, flickering light, the flaming heart of the world glowing up through the bowels of the volcano. Peering over the edge, Ram could see, and I saw with him, rosy pools of fiery lava far below, sluggishly tossing and stirring. Gusts of hot wind rose from them. And, staring down into that distant churning furnace, I saw the death of Atlantis waiting to burst loose.

Here he crouched, head pressed against his knees. Here he prayed to be liberated from the spirit that had invaded him.

He named the names of gods. He named the names of kings—the secret names, the names they had worn as princes, before they became the newest Harinamur. He called upon all the forces of the universe to free him from—

Me.

The words came pouring out of him in a wild, keening howl, weird and strange-sounding. "I have strayed from the path of my fathers," he cried, sobbing. "I know not how, but I have sinned, and I have been punished for my sin, and now I am accursed. Tell me my penitence, O gods! Tell me how I can set myself free!"

And knelt there, shivering in the volcanic heat, waiting for the grace of his gods to descend upon him.

For one crazy instant I actually thought it was going to work—that I would be scraped from his mind and hurled into some unthinkable limbo. It was terrifying. Whirlwinds swooped and roared about me. The walls of the chamber seemed to be closing in on me. The mountain was pressing down.

Ram seemed completely in charge, Ram and his gods. I could feel him searching around for me, trying to get a grip on me and pry me loose.

I had to fight like a—well, like a demon. I pushed him away from me, set up defense blocks around myself, fled down the corridors of his mind. There were moments when I felt him seizing me, prying me free, thrusting me out.

I suppose there must have been some way for me to take control of his mind and keep him at bay, but just then that didn't seem possible. I was on the run. For one long scary moment down there in that sweltering room in the belly of the mountain, he had the upper hand and I was helpless. I hunkered down tight and tried to make myself very small within him, invisible, unfindable.

And the moment passed. I reached out and linked myself to his mind again, and found the levers of control. I felt the pressure ease. I was the rider again, and he was the vehicle. I was safe.

The whirlwinds died away. Everything that had been crowding close upon me now retreated. After a time Ram rose from his crouch.

He was very calm—relaxed, even. Did he think he had succeeded in expelling me? Perhaps. Perhaps. Or maybe he was simply content to have come so close to victory over me. He swung his arms cheerfully, he stretched his legs, he filled his lungs, like an athlete who has just completed a grueling match and is beginning to unwind.

And started back up the winding passageway, feeling his way quickly, carving by carving, until in a surprisingly short time he had reached the mouth of the cavern.

As he stepped out into the bright afternoon sunlight he said—inwardly, speaking directly to me—

—*So even the Labyrinth is of no avail.*

His words hit me like blows.

You have not fooled me, demon! I know you are still there. But I will not let you rule me. I will not let you be my master.

There was a strange new strength flowing from him. He was determined now to fight me to the finish, and I knew it.

Can he possibly do it?

He's strong and tough. But I know how to operate his mind, and he doesn't know how to operate mine. Not really. He was close, back there in the Labyrinth, but not close enough.

Still, I could feel him resisting me when I put him in trance to write this last section of this very long letter. I was able to win out, of course. But the next time it could be a lot harder. I have a real tiger on my hands.

The situation looks messy. I'll try to keep you posted. That may not be so easy, though.

—Roy

□ E I G H T □

Day 18, Western Wind, Great River.

Where I left things in the last letter, it all seemed pretty dire. But actually I've had a few days of respite. Much to my surprise, Prince Ram has been behaving as though the exorcism in the Labyrinth really did work and the evil spirit has been cast forth from his soul. At least, that's what he told Counsellor Teneristis when he returned to the palace later that day. And he hasn't tried to aim any more direct communications my way.

I have these four explanations for the way he's acting:

1) He really has convinced himself that the exorcism must have worked, despite what he said to me as we were coming out of the cavern.

2) He's trying to fake me out, so that he can blindside me when he thinks my guard is down.

3) He's afraid that Teneristis, upon hearing that the Labyrinth didn't do the job, will send him off on

some even more dangerous and strenuous pilgrimage that he really doesn't want to undertake.

4) With the Rite of Anointing coming up very shortly—the grand ceremony by which Prince Ram becomes virtual co-monarch with his father—he simply doesn't want to have to deal with the distraction of thinking about the demon that may or may not be possessing him.

Any or all of these four may be correct. Or none.

If Ram really thinks I'm gone, why did he tell me that he knows I'm still here? Doesn't make sense. Nor can I easily believe that he's afraid of Teneristis, or of any new penitence that Teneristis might saddle him with. The Prince didn't seem at all hesitant about going into the Labyrinth. What could possibly be worse than that?

The theory about the Rite of Anointing has a little more substance. It's the biggest event of his life so far. What if it's dangerous in some way, or blasphemous, to try to undergo the rite while you're possessed by a demon? Maybe Ram's so eager for the Anointing that he doesn't want the rite postponed, which might happen if he let Teneristis know that he's still carrying that stubborn demon around in his head. On the other hand, Ram is honorable, above all else. Can he honorably conceal the fact that the exorcism didn't work, and let himself go through with this immensely significant ceremony while he's in a ritually impure state?

That leaves #2, which unfortunately seems all too plausible. Ram has been trained to be a king, and that involves being crafty. If there's a pesky enemy bothering you who won't go away, one way to handle him would be to lay low and clobber him when he's not expecting it.

There's also the possibility that Ram's worried that this whole demonic possession business could lead to his being disqualified to become king at all, that he might be passed over in favor of his younger brother, unless he sweeps the entire thing under the carpet as fast as he can.

Whatever the reason, the Prince is keeping quiet these days. And so am I.

Three hours later. And everything is completely different now. Just for starters, let me tell you that the Prince is not in a trance as I write this. He's completely conscious, aware of what's going on, though of course he has no idea of the meaning of the words that his hand is shaping under my control.

I may be making the worst mistake of my life. And the *last* mistake of my life, too. But somehow I think everything is going to be all right. Let me tell you what happened.

The thing that kicked it off was the arrival of the diplomatic pouch from Naz Glesim. It contained the second of your letters, the one in which you talk about the mammoth hunt. (I think they have to be nuts to go out hunting gigantic beasts like that in the middle of a driving snowstorm. Even if they do believe that warm weather will never come unless they do it.) As before, the scroll was packed as if it had come from Provincial Governor Sippurilayl and was addressed to Prince Ram, so the bureaucrats downstairs brought it straight to the Prince in his study.

This time the Prince waited until they were gone before opening it. I waited, too, figuring I'd pounce on him and put him in trance just as he started to unroll it, so that he wouldn't even have a phantom memory of once again having glimpsed something written in English. But he was way ahead of me.

Without unrolling it, he said, aiming the thought right at me, sharp and fierce as a lightning-bolt:

—*Does this contain more of your demon-writing?*

So he knew I was still there. I remained silent and tried to seem inconspicuous. Didn't help.

—*Tell me. What is this all about? Is there a demon inside Provincial Governor Sippurilayl also? What do you two demons say to each other in your letters?*

Then he opened the scroll and stared at it.

—*Yes,* he said. *As I thought. More demon-marks. Very well, demon. I am unable to expel you; therefore, I must attempt to know you. Tell me who and what you are, demon. I command you to reply. By all the gods do I command you!*

I was at a crossroads. I could have knocked him out then and there, and tried once more to edit from his mind all recollection of this latest scroll. Or I could admit the truth—despite everything that our training says—and see what would happen next.

Lora, I didn't hesitate more than a fraction of a second.

—I am not a demon, I said. *I am a visitor from a land that lies far away at the other end of time.*

I said it. I actually said it. I gave away the whole show.

I didn't feel that I had any other option, Lora. Probably we never should have started sending these letters back and forth; but we did—I take the blame for that—and so the Prince and most likely Provincial Governor Sippurilayl also have been exposed to the sight of documents written in English. And the Prince, at least, has managed to figure out that something peculiar is going on.

I suppose I could, even at this point, have gone into Prince Ram's mind and tried to carve out every bit of data having to do with my presence there and with the scrolls he had seen. But I hadn't done such a great job of editing his mind in my previous attempts, apparently, and there was so much now to remove that I didn't for a moment think I could do it without seriously damaging him.

I wasn't going to risk that.

Better to break all the rules, and tell him the full truth, and take the consequences, both here and in Home Era, for what I had done.

And what was the Prince's reaction, do you think? Bewilderment? Shock? Horror? Or a simple snort of anger and derision at the thought that the demon who was infesting him was a *crazy* demon, thus making a bad situation worse?

None of the above. He wasn't annoyed or upset. He was very calm, matter-of-fact, almost casual. I suppose that is one of the differences between ordinary mortals and princes who have been trained all their lives to be rulers of a great realm. Your basic prince needs to know how to stay cool and collected in the face of any sort of crisis, no matter how weird.

He said, *So you come from the time when the gods walked the earth? That golden time long ago?*

—*No. I come from a time yet unborn.*

—*A future time, you mean?*

—*The future, yes. More than twenty thousand years from now.*

—*Ah. How very strange. And are you of our people?*

I hesitated. —*I don't think so. No.*

He thought about that. —*Of the Dirt People, then?*

—*Perhaps. I can't be certain.*

—*Because you come from such a distant time?*

—*Yes*, I said. *In twenty thousand years many things change.*

His mental voice was silent a long while. I felt him pondering the information I had given him, examining it, mulling it, digesting it.

At last he said, *If you come from so far away, then you must be a great wizard.*

—*Not really. But great wizards sent me here.*

—*You are no wizard? You are only a demon?*

—*Neither a demon nor a wizard, Prince Ram.*

He said, after considering that a moment, *I think you are a wizard all the same. What is your name, wizard?*

—*Roy Colton.*

—*That is a name only a wizard would have.*

—*It's a very ordinary name, I assure you.*

—It is a wizard's name, the Prince replied firmly. *I have no doubt of that.* He was still completely calm. *And why have you entered my mind, wizard? What is it you seek there?*

The tone of his mental voice was casual, conversational. It unsettled me a little, the ease with which he seemed to be accepting my presence within him now. Knowing about it had upset him at first, sure, but he didn't appear to have any problem with it now. He seemed to find it pretty interesting. He was curious about the whys and wherefores.

Was he setting a trap for me?

It didn't look that way. I took a readout on his endocrine systems and saw that beneath his pose of calmness lay nothing but more calmness. You or I, discovering that some inexplicable phantom has taken residence in our heads, would never have been so calm. We'd have figured we were going psycho and checked ourselves into the nearest ward for a complete workover. But that's the value, I guess, of living in a world where the gods are still real and vivid and where you expect to run into the occasional demon or wizard now and then. It didn't occur to Prince Ram that he might have lost his sanity when he started hearing voices in his head. My being inside him was simply a challenge that had to be dealt with, a problem that had to be solved.

His openness and straightforwardness were tremendously appealing. He simply wanted to know who I was and what my being here was all about.

So I told him everything. I broke every rule in the book.

I told him how in the distant future land where I lived, we had developed the power to send our minds backward in time. I described the way time research had begun, the first experiments, the failures and the successes, the early short-hop attempts at going back a few hours, a few days, a few weeks. I went on to talk about how, as we mastered the technique, we'd begun to send volunteers back across the centuries in the form of disembodied consciousnesses—jumping a hundred years, five hundred, a thousand.

Whether he really understood very much of this is anybody's guess. But from the fluctuations of his hormone levels I could tell that he was spellbound, utterly fascinated, when I spoke of the way time explorers, reporting on their experiences, are able to recapture the past and make it seem to live again.

And then I spoke of Athilan—"Atlantis, as we call it," I said. I described how, as we pushed our research back and back and back, we began picking up sketchy details of the existence of Athilan, and I told him that of all the nations of the ancient world, the empire of Athilan was the greatest, and therefore was the one that we yearned most to know about.

I held my breath, afraid that I'd given away too much. I didn't want to have to tell him of the coming destruction of his land, the obliteration of all but the most hazy memory of the great empire that was Athilan. But I had tossed him a big hint, of course. If

Athilan was all but forgotten in my time, what was I saying, if not that it had been destroyed somewhere along the way? But he was so interested in the idea of consciousnesses wandering back in time that we went right by that obvious point.

—*Are you the first wizard of your people to visit Athilan?* he asked.

—*The third,* I said. And I told him of Fletcher's pioneering trip, and Iversen's, and how the information they brought back was useful in its way but too limited, because Fletcher had landed in the mind of a slave, and Iversen in that of a not very bright shopkeeper, and neither one was capable of providing much insight into the details of Athilantan life. So a deliberate attempt was made, I said, to see to it that the next explorer who went back to Athilan entered the mind of a member of the ruling family.

—*And here you are,* Prince Ram said.

—*And here I am.*

We talked half the afternoon, through what would normally have been his exercise period. He overflowed with questions about the world I came from.

I described telephones for him, and television, and supersonic transports, and space satellites. I told him that we had mining camps on the Moon and three little scientific outposts on Mars, and were talking about sending a crew out for a close look at the moons of Jupiter. I made a stab at explaining what our system of government is like, and what it's like to live in a world that has several great nations instead of only one, and how we managed to survive the ferocious conflicts that almost finished us all off in the horrendous twentieth century.

He wasn't skeptical in the slightest. I guess he had no trouble believing that wizards capable of sending a man's mind back twenty thousand years could also make machines that could fly from Thibarak to Naz Glesim in a couple of hours, or send pictures halfway around the world in a moment.

The only thing he absolutely couldn't swallow was the notion of democratic elections. He wanted to know the name of our king, and how long he and his family had ruled.

—*It doesn't work that way any more, I said. In our land we choose a new ruler every four years. If he or she rules wisely, they are often given four years more. And then we choose someone else.*

That made no sense to him, no matter how many different ways I explained it.

The *people* choose the king? A *stranger* is allowed to replace an established ruler?

He was baffled. His body grew tense, his head began to throb. Only when I told him that there were other countries where the rulers held power for a great many years, sometimes for their whole lives, did he ease back a little.

But even the concept of dictatorship seemed bizarre and troublesome to him. To grab power and proclaim yourself the boss, and then to rule until the people grow tired of you and overthrow you, whereupon somebody else stands up and says he's boss—no, no, Prince Ram couldn't swallow that. It seemed like insanity to him. Our scientific wonders, our television and time travel and voyages to Mars, those he could accept without a quiver of doubt. But not our politics.

Wrapping it up, the next day.

Where it stands now is that Ram and I have become pals. The best of friends. He completely accepts my presence within him, is not at all spooked by it, thinks it's just terrific. A wizard from the far future living behind his forehead who can tell him all sorts of marvelous things. Doesn't intend to let anyone know about it, naturally. His little secret, to cherish and enjoy.

I realize that this violates all our training, for me to have let him in on the truth of the situation. It goes against everything that we're taught in the way of procedural tactics. My neck's going to be on the block for sure when I return to Home Era. So all this has big implications not just for my future, but for yours and mine together. Don't think I haven't been troubled by that. But I couldn't help doing what I've done. It was the only honorable choice. Either admit the truth, or risk destroying Prince Ram's sanity. Well, I made my choice, and now I have to stick with it, even though it certainly means the ruination of my career.

He knows that you're occupying the mind of Provincial Governor Sippurilayl. He knows that we communicate by means of these letters, and he will continue to oblige me by serving as my scribe. Whether you want to reveal yourself to Sippurilayl is entirely up to you. Personally I don't think you

should. You have nothing to gain from it and everything to lose once you're back in Home Era. After
all, you still have a career in time research to think
about, regardless of the mess I've made of mine.

Will you go on writing to me, knowing what
you know now?

I hope you will. I'll be devastated if you don't,
Lora.

Please don't worry that by corresponding with
me you'll be making yourself some kind of accom-
plice in my breach of the rules. I'm going to let it be
known loud and clear, when we've returned to Home
Era, that I chose to make my presence known to
Ram entirely on my own, without consulting you
and certainly without any suggestion from you that I
do it.

As you know, I never *intended* to blow my cover
this way. It was just something that happened. To
do it was wrong, and I'm prepared to take the consequences, whatever they may be, when the time
comes. I have to say, though, that I don't really see
what harm it does, this far in the past, to let one
clever prince know that we of the twenty-first century are capable of roving through time. His knowing that can't possibly change any aspect of history,
can it?

Or can it?

Well, so be it, What I've done can't be undone.
Ram kept himself up half the night talking with me,
asking a million and one questions, the way you
would with a new college roommate. All about my
family, the place where I was born, my training as a

"wizard," et cetera, et cetera, et cetera, until he was goofy with fatigue and I had to ease him to sleep without his knowing it, for his own sake.

Roommates is what we are, all right.

How strange this all is, Lora! How totally strange.

—Roy

□ N I N E □

DAY 22, WESTERN WIND, GREAT RIVER.

News. Big news. A flabbergasting, mind-blowing discovery, in fact. A completely unexpected discovery that makes everything that was impossible to explain about the Athilantan empire fall suddenly into place.

Now that I no longer need to conceal my presence from Ram, I can move about freely in his mind. That doesn't seem to bother him. He doesn't see it as an invasion of his privacy; he doesn't seem to understand the concept of privacy at all. Or care about it, if he does.

One thing I wanted to know about was the rite of Romany Star.

Remember that mysterious ceremony that Ram and his father performed one night last month? The Prince and the King staring at the sky, chanting solemn prayers to one particular star, shredding and burning their garments, destroying the coronets that they wore? Obviously an important rite. But what was its significance?

I slipped down into the depths of Ram's consciousness to see what I could learn about it. And got a lot more than I was expecting.

As I hardly need to tell you, you can't do research in a human mind, whether it's your own or someone else's, the way you would in a public library. Minds have no indexes and you can't run a computer scan to find the particular data you want. Everything is arranged systematically inside the mind, I suppose, but the genius has not yet been born who is capable of figuring out what that system is. So the best you can do is poke around randomly and try to make the connections you need.

I touched here and there within Ram's mind, looking for the memories of the night of the Romany Star rite. I came up with all sorts of other things—the time in the Labyrinth, and a stroll along a spectacular beach, all white sands and sparkling water, and a wild horseback ride down some forest glade, and so on and so on—and then there it was, Ram and the King on the palace roof chanting their prayer.

That entry in Ram's memory file had a special feel to it, a distinct resonance, a tone all its own. It was like one of those haunting melodies that you couldn't possibly sing yourself, but which you'd recognize whenever you heard it. I can't describe it to you, but I know what it was like. And, now that I had experienced it, I had a reference point. I went darting off down this mental avenue and that one, hoping to pick that special tone up again somewhere else, another point of association with Romany Star.

And I found it. It came rising up toward me out of a part of his brain where history and myth lay sleeping. Intermingled with it was a strange bleak image: charred debris, bits of burned rope, twisted fragments of what looked like hammocks, rising out of a sea of ashes. I looked closer. I felt dry hot winds. I saw a great swollen red sun in the sky.

Closer. Deeper. The ashes rose and became an eerie city made of woven reeds. Buildings, streets, bridges—everything light, delicate, insubstantial. Somber-faced people walked in silence through its narrow, interlacing lanes. Sometimes it was night, and a string of shining moons was hung across the sky. Then came day, and that gigantic menacing sun.

The people had the look of the people of Athilan: dark hair and eyes, dark complexions, stocky bodies, broad shoulders. I thought I saw Ram in those streets, and his father.

The sun grew larger. The air grew hotter. There was terror in the eyes of the people who walked in the streets. Their world was coming to an end. Soon fire would sweep through the sky; soon this delicate city of woven reeds would become the sea of ashes that I had been shown before.

I saw ships lifting off into space. Maybe a dozen or more of them, carrying the lucky few, chosen by lot, who would escape the explosion of the red sun.

And the rest—the rest—oh, Lora, I knew what would happen to them, and my heart ached for them! A whole world destroyed. Romany Star sending spears of flame across the gulf of space, and everything perishing, everything except what was aboard those twelve or sixteen starships.

The moment of devastation came. Terrible light, like the fury of a thousand nuclear bombs at once, burst overhead. But the starships were on their way, up and out, heading into the vast darkness that lay beyond the blazing sky.

Do you understand what I'm saying, Lora?

Lora, these Athilantans are *aliens*. Humanoid aliens, so much like humans that it's just about impossible to tell the difference. They came here aboard those starships, refugees from some other world light-years away that died when its sun went nova.

No wonder they're head and shoulders above the real natives of the Paleolithic world. Maybe a thousand years before the era that you and I are visiting now, maybe three thousand, they dropped down suddenly out of space, bringing to a world that didn't yet know the use of metals a culture that could build spaceships capable of traveling between the stars. That is, a culture that's advanced even beyond our own.

To the Cro-Magnons and their contemporaries, they must have seemed like gods. In a way they *were* gods. And they built a mighty city in the midst of Earth's frostbound Stone Age darkness.

Their descendants here in Athilan still look back in sorrow and anguish to their old lost home, which they call Romany Star. On a certain night each year they turn their eyes to the stars, and they chant the prayer for the dead, in remembrance of all that had been theirs before the red sun swelled in the sky, before their unstable home star flared up and destroyed their world.

Now I understand why the people of Athilan gave thanks for Ram's return to the human realm when he came back to the city from the mainland, and why they refer to the mainlanders as the Dirt People.

I suppose they could have found some more complimentary term for them than that, but the fact remains that the Athilantans see themselves as the only true humans, and the mainlanders, the natives of Earth, as some sort of inferior alien beings. It isn't really the sort of racism that used to be so common in our modern world. That involved one branch of the human species telling itself that it was superior to the other branches of the human race. There wasn't any justification for those feelings of superiority. All the different races of modern Earth are just minor variations of the same species, *Homo sapiens*. But these people *really are superior*. And they aren't simply a special branch of *Homo sapiens*. They aren't *Homo sapiens* at all, even though they look just like us, or nearly so. They're a different species entirely. I'm not saying it's admirable or pretty in any way for them to have such contempt for the mainlanders. But at least I can understand why they feel that way. And also I think that when we translate their words into ours the terms they use may come out sounding a little more contemptuous than the Athilantans actually intend.

Doesn't it all sound completely crazy? Refugees from the stars, traveling here on spaceborne arks, founding a glorious city on this balmy isle in the eastern Atlantic, and setting up a far-flung Paleolithic empire? But it's true. I've located Ram's memories of the historical chronicles that he studied when he was a boy. You can probably find the same stuff in Sippurilayl's mind if you look for it.

And now we know why these people are so improbably far ahead of everyone else who existed on Earth in prehistoric times. They had a tremendous head start.

The present-day Athilantan civilization isn't nearly as advanced as the one that died with Romany Star. They've lost a lot of their old technological knowledge over the centuries, perhaps through neglect, or maybe simply because they weren't able to reconstruct it on this new world. But they're still inconceivably superior in abilities and attainments to the primitive hunting folk over whom they rule.

It *does* sound too fantastic to be true. A myth, a legend, a poem, anything but the actual truth.

Well, it *is* the actual truth. I absolutely believe that. I've discussed it with Ram and he vehemently insists that it isn't any myth—that it all really happened, the solar flare that destroyed their world, the migration to Earth, the building of Athilan on an uninhabited island in the warmest part of the planet. They have detailed and reliable chronicles describing the whole thing. Every child studies the history of the calamity the way we study Christopher Columbus and George Washington.

Go check out Provincial Governor Sippurilayl's memories of his childhood history lessons. You'll find it all there. I know that you will.

And what a tremendous story it is, isn't it?

—Roy

□ T E N □

DAY 4, MONTH OF GOLDEN DAYS, Year of Great River.

I hope you haven't been worried about me during my long silence. Everything's fine here. I just haven't felt much like writing letters.

The truth is I've been a little embarrassed about my last two letters, the one in which I confess that I've revealed my presence to Ram, and the one in which I tell you about my discovery of the extraterrestrial origin of the Athilantans. (Have you received that second one yet? You'll be awfully confused by what I've just said if you haven't.) I was afraid that one or the other of those letters would convince you that I'd gone loony—that you'd write back to me full of fury about my breaking of the time-travel rules, or that you'd tell me that the business about the Athilantans coming from a different solar system was the craziest nonsense you had ever heard. So I couldn't bring myself to send you any more

□ 109

letters until I saw what your reaction to those two was.

Well, now your reply to my I've-told-Ram-everything letter has come in. I'm immensely relieved that you aren't angry with me, Lora. It makes me realize all over again what a wonderful person you are. And why I love you so much.

No question, as you say, that I'm going to be in very hot water when I get back to Home Era. But you do recognize, as I hoped you would, that letting Ram know the truth was my only honorable course. I simply couldn't let the heir to the throne go on thinking he was possessed by a demon, and calling in all sorts of witch-doctors to exorcise him.

You don't comment on the other and bigger revelation, from which I conclude that you haven't seen my second letter yet, though you'll be able to figure out something of what it's about from what I've said here. In any case I can tell you that I've done a lot of further research—Ram has taken me through the royal archives, which contain extremely elaborate records of every event in Athilantan history—and I have no doubt at all that the interstellar-migration story is accurate. Ram and his people really do come from another world.

The Athilantans have been on Earth for 1143 years. Harinamur—the first one—was the captain of the space fleet that brought them here. The migration took them only thirty-one years, which means they must have traveled at the speed of light, or something pretty close to it. That implies a technology way beyond ours, at least so far as space travel goes, since we haven't managed yet to reach speeds anything like that and we're still limited to our own Solar System. For the time being, anyway.

Sixteen starships altogether made the trip. They don't exist any more—they were dismantled and totally recycled into other things during the early years of the colony, when metals were scarce. When they landed here, they knew they were here to stay: they weren't going to be journeying between the stars ever again.

It ought to be possible for the people up front to check all this out by running an astronomical survey. There can't be many red stars within a 31-light-year radius that have a history of instability, and maybe they can figure out which one of them went nova about 20,000 B.C. And then we'd know where Romany Star was. When we become capable of building spaceships fast enough to travel to other stars, which I guess is still another hundred years or so ahead for us, we can send an expedition out to look for the charred ruins of the civilization that once lived there, and confirm that whole thing.

On to other matters.

The Prince and I are getting along very well. He's completely comfortable with the idea that we share the same body. As he goes through his day's princely chores he keeps a running commentary going, explaining everything that he's doing. I've learned vast amounts about the trade routes of the Athilantan empire, about its history, about its religion. I hope I can keep it all straight in my head until I get back to Home Era. (*Damn* not having any way to take notes back with us! But at least they did a good job of training us to use our memories.)

The Prince questions me, too, about Home Era. Our time is like a fantasy to him—a time when billions of people occupy the Earth and all sorts of different cultures exist—and his appetite for details about it is tremendous. He wants to know about city planning, about our arts and religions, about sports, about automobiles and airplanes, about almost anything. I think he suspects that I'm making up some or even all of what I tell him. There are moments it almost feels like that to me: Home Era seems terribly far away, terribly unreal. After these months here I sometimes think that only Athilan is real and everything else is a fairy tale. Having no body of your own will do that to you, I've heard.

A big event lies just ahead: the Rite of Anointing. Preparations are already in full swing and the whole city is involved in them.

You will recall that this is the third of the four major rites that a prince must undergo, following the Rite of Designation and the Rite of Joining, before he is ready to become Grand Darionis of Athilan. Apparently in this one the heir to the throne receives certain great revelations that every king must know. What these revelations might be, Ram has no idea. But the prospect of finally finding out has him terrifically excited.

Me too, I have to say.

It's another few weeks, now. We're both going to have a tough time waiting for the days to pass.

The one thing I'm afraid of now is that the folks

back at Home Year are going to give me the hook just before the rite. That really upsets me; knowing that the clock is ticking all the time. And then I'll never find out what the mysteries were.

How much more time here do I really have? That's the big question. I don't know. You remember in one of my first letters I told you that I had lost track of the count of Home Era days. The information you sent helped a little, but not enough. I may be as much as a week off in my count. On top of that, it's unclear to me what the exact day when they're supposed to pull me back is. "Six months," they said, but do they mean that right down to the day, or is it just a rough figure? So I might have another two weeks here, a month, maybe even six weeks. I can't tell. And I want to stay here as long as I can, Lora. For obvious reasons I'm not looking forward to going back there and facing the music. But aside from that I simply don't want to leave. Not yet. Not until I've learned everything I can possibly learn about this place. And I have a feeling that the Rite of Anointing is going to tell me plenty.

Hope to hear from you soon.

With all my love—

—Roy

□ ELEVEN □

Another long silence from me, I know. I was holding off, so I could describe the Rite of Anointing to you. Well, the Rite of Anointing has now taken place—it was three days ago. The mysteries have been revealed. It was a tremendous event—and also tremendously upsetting. A fantastic experience. Completely overwhelming, the kind of thing that takes absolute possession of you and won't let go. Both Prince Ram and I were pretty badly shaken up by it all. And so I've needed a few days just to think about what happened, to come to terms with it, to understand my own reactions and feelings. I'm not sure I really have a handle on it even now.

Let me see—where should I start?

At the beginning, I guess. The morning of the day of the Rite of Anointing. It was one of those magnificent springlike Athilantan days, warm golden sunlight, clear crisp blue sky, that make the fact that we are actually living in the Ice Age seem like such a joke. (Every day is springtime in Athilan. Something like the best days California can do, but even lovelier.)

The Prince had fasted all the previous day, and had stayed awake all through the night, praying and chanting. We had no contact with each other. I took care to keep myself well below the threshold of his consciousness. Obviously he didn't want to be disturbed, and I didn't want to disturb him.

At dawn, his personal slaves led him to the great marble bath chamber of the palace, and bathed and anointed him with perfumes and oils. They dressed him then, in a magnificent robe of pure white cotton bordered in purple richly brocaded and trimmed with cloth of gold. From the bath chamber he went to a small, very austere chapel on the ground floor, where for a time he prayed in front of column of shining black stone.

Now his family came to him: first his sister Princess Rayna, then his younger brother Prince Caiminor, and then his mother, Queen Aliralin, whom I hadn't encountered before. (A slender, stately, very queenly woman of great beauty. She had been on the north shore of the island, it seems, in a religious retreat.)

As they went before Prince Ram, each one knelt to him, even his mother, and with outstretched hands silently offered him a shallow cup of polished pink stone that contained a small quantity of some aromatic wine. He sipped very solemnly. One wine was ruby red, one was golden, one scarcely had any color at all. Each affected him in a slightly different way. The overall effect was not one of making him drunk—the wines of Athilan don't seem to make anybody drunk—but nevertheless transforming his spirit, giving it a glow, a radiance, that it had not had before.

Then his father came to him, bareheaded but clad in the most sumptuous royal robe imaginable, deep purple with great flaring shoulder-pieces of rich scarlet, and loomed before him like a god. He didn't speak a word, but simply extended his hand to Ram, drew him from the chapel, walked with him out of the palace and down those myriad steps to the great plaza out front. A chariot was waiting, drawn by two of the fierce, snorting little horses that the Athilantans use.

The entire population of the city, so it seemed, had turned out to see the royal procession go by. The route was a grand circle through the city. We went westward, first, down the Concourse of the Sky almost as far as the waterfront, then around to the north along a broad curving boulevard, paved with shining pink flagstones, called the Avenue of the Gods. There were cheering crowds everywhere, calling out to Ram.

"Thilayl!" they yelled. "Highness!"

And also: "Stolifar Blayl!" Which is part of his secret formal name, and means "Light of the Universe," and apparently is only spoken aloud on the Day of Anointing.

The purpose of the procession, which took hours, was simply to display Ram to the populace. By midday, we were back almost exactly where we had started, in the zone of temples and palaces at the center of the place. The sun was high and bright, now, glinting off the white stone facades of Athilan.

We went around to the eastern side of the sacred district, where the land starts to slope up toward the foothills of Mount Balamoris. Here, overlooking the entire city, is the glorious Plaza of a Thousand Columns, one of the most magnificent public spaces any city ever had. Just beyond the north side of the plaza stands an unassuming, windowless little building made of big blocks of black granite. This is the House of the Anointing, where royal powers are conferred on the members of the ruling family of Athilan.

Walking barefoot, side by side, Ram and his father went in. It was dark within except for a single shaft of noonday light that pierced a twelve-sided opening in the ceiling. The King formally touched fingertips with his son, and they embraced; and then, without a word, the King left the building.

Ram knelt beneath that shaft of light.

Three figures in priestly robes appeared from the darkness beyond. Smooth white masks, unbroken except for tiny eye-slits, completely hid their faces. They loomed above the kneeling Ram and lightly brushed his forehead with a thick, sweet oil. The Anointing, this was. Then they commenced a slow rhythmic chant, speaking in the ancient form of the Athilantan language which is used for epic poetry and religious scriptures, and which—like Latin in our own day—hardly anyone here really understands. Certainly Ram was able to comprehend just a few scattered phrases—all cliches, things about his high royal heritage, the grave responsibilities that were to be his, et cetera, et cetera.

Then, just as his sister and brother and mother had done much earlier that day, each priest in turn offered Ram a shallow bowl of polished stone to drink from. The wine, if wine it was, had a light, spicy taste, and it was giving off gentle fizzy bubbles.

The priests withdrew.

Ram knelt, head down, waiting.

Slowly, slowly, slowly, a dreamlike state began to take possession of his mind. A darkness, a dizziness, overtook him. The narrow golden beam from above grew dim. Swirls of color swept back and forth like waves, like billowing curtains, in the black depths of the House of Anointing.

Visions came to him.

Everything was turbulent and unclear at first. Then his mind became a screen, and he saw, and I saw with him, the night sky, the vastness of space, meteors rushing past, stars and galaxies, great surging comets.

The focus changed. Now his mind drifted down to the surface of the old world of Romany Star, as it had been before its destruction. The wickerwork houses, the streets of woven reeds, everything supple and pliant, shifting in the slightest breezes. And the people of Romany Star quietly going about their tasks, living busily, happily—

Until the sun began to swell, until that great red eye came to fill the heavens—

Motionless, impassive, Prince Ram and I watched

once again the destruction of his people's original world. The prayers, the outcries, the dry wind, the scorching heat, the first pale puff of flame, the smoldering houses, and then the holocaust, a world afire, everything transformed into ashes in a moment, while the sixteen gleaming starships rose desperately into the heavens with their little load of lucky escapees—

The migration, then, we watched. The years of wandering through space, searching for a habitable planet. The first wondrous glimpse of Earth, blue and shining in the black bowl of night. The survey party landing, going forth across the bleak chilly continents to find a place where the Athilantans might live. The discovery of the warm lovely isle lapped by a kindly ocean. The sixteen ships plunging downward, bringing the wanderers at last to their new home.

Prince Ram and I were eye-witnesses, within a span of just moments, to the entire history of his race. The wine, the drug, whatever it was that had been in those shallow stone bowls, had cut him free from the bonds of the time-line, and he drifted untethered through the ages, roaming the whole past without restraint, without boundary.

We saw the city being built. Harinamur the One King, the original one, amidst his people, laying out the avenues and boulevards, selecting the sites for the temples, the palaces, the parks, the marketplaces. Workers using cunning devices swiftly carving slabs of marble from the hillsides. This city would be nothing like the old lost home on Romany Star.

There, everything had been lithe, delicate, yielding. Here they would build of stone.

The city arose. And the people of Athilan went forth from it into the frosty hinterlands beyond, and made themselves known to the savage people who dwelled there, and built an empire linked by the first roads and the first ships this world had ever seen.

We watched the city grow. We watched it flourish. Brilliant sunlight glinting off the palaces of white stone. Magnificent villas climbing the green slopes of Mount Balamoris. The harbor crowded with ships, bearing goods from every quarter of this splendid untouched planet.

And then—then everything changed. In a moment. In the twinkling of an eye.

First came a darkening of the sky. Then a strand of black smoke rising from the summit of the mountain. A sudden tremor underfoot. I was caught without warning by the shift in the tone of the vision. Ram, deep in his dreams of the past, had no idea at all of what was coming. But, after a moment, I did.

I saw now that in the Anointing he was able to wander both forward and backward in time. He had had a vision of this great city's founding. And now he was going to be shown its doom.

Oh, Lora, if I could have spared him the sight! If I could have covered his eyes and kept him from seeing the death of Athilan, I tell you I would have done it! But I had no power. I was only an insignificant passenger crammed into a corner of his dreaming mind.

And so we watched it together.

The flames bursting from the mountain. The smoke staining the pure clear sky a dirty dingy gray. The sudden rainfall of small light pumice stones clattering down everywhere. Then the thick clouds of ash bursting forth. The mighty tremors running through the ground. Huge slabs of marble dropping form the facades of buildings. The columns of the Plaza of the Thousand Columns moving crazily from side to side, then tumbling as if struck by the side of a giant's hand.

The earth shaking—heaving—splitting open—streets cracking, houses falling, pavements vanishing into newly created abysses—

The sky turning black—

The sea rising—

A great terrifying groaning sound filling the air, coming not from the throats of the populace but from the earth itself. Flames everywhere. The roar of the water as it rushes forward onto the land. Lava spilling down the sides of the mountain and pouring into the city. Earthquake, flood, volcanic eruption, everything at once. Destruction on all sides. Doom. Doom. Doom.

A few ships putting out from the harbor, struggling against the fantastic heaving of the waves. A pitiful band of refugees, once again setting forth to save themselves as Athilan is brought down into ruin, just as Romany Star once had been.

The surface of the land subsides. It just drops downward into itself, as if everything that had been supporting it had gone up in the eruption. The sea comes pouring in, and nothing can hold it back.

There's a different sound now, a strange taut high-pitched one, like the thrumming of some immense insect, growing louder, louder, louder, until it fills every space and there can be room for nothing else anywhere in the world. It's the sound of the city dying. And then it stops, with awful abruptness, with a *crack* of silence followed by a great stillness.

The stillness goes on and on.

The sky is clear again, blue with a golden sun, and the hugeness of the sea spreads before us.

Of the island of Athilan there is not the slightest sign. It has been devoured; it has been swallowed up; it has vanished beneath the surface of the water as though it had never existed.

The vision ended. Ram didn't move. He knelt there as though he'd been clubbed. Through his numbed mind there ran, again and again, ghastly scenes out of the last hour of Athilan.

Then the door of the House of Anointing opened, and the three masked priests returned. With them was the King. He wore no mask; and his face was stark and stern as he knelt over his son and drew him gently to his feet. From his look, I realized that the King knew what Ram had seen. He had seen it himself, years before, on the day of his own Anointing.

So this is the mystery that the princes of this empire are shown as they enter into full manhood. They are pulled loose from the framework of time—how, I can't even guess—and allowed to float freely, backward and then forward. And they are shown the fate that awaits this greatest of all cities.

What a shattering thing to learn! To discover that all striving is in vain, that discipline and ambition, hard work and planning, prayers and rituals, lead only to fiery doom and watery destruction! Why, then, bother to take on the burdens of being a king? Everything is pointless. Nothing you achieve can possibly withstand the coming fury. Your homeland will sink beneath the sea and be forgotten. What a devastating lesson that is!

No wonder Ram had crouched there in a stupor of shock and defeat.

When he left the House of Anointing with his father and the three priests he walked as a prince must walk, straight-backed, square-shouldered. But his eyes were bleak and his mind still lay locked in gloom and torment and cold despair. And that's how he has been, these three days past. A cloud of seemingly unbreakable depression hangs over him. He won't speak to anyone, he doesn't eat at all, he remains in his room.

I can't say I feel a lot better myself. The waves of sorrow and amazement and horror that come from Ram's mind have seeped into my own, and my mood is gray and chilly. There's no use trying to kid myself with cheery little uplifting cliches. I've been forced right up against the underlying truth of things. What a dark and cruel place the world is, for all its beauty, for all its wonder! We have miracles around us on every side—a *spiderweb* is a miracle, Lora!—but also we have violence, insanity, terrible disease, sudden death. The same Nature that brings us the mountains and the rivers and the green glistening meadows brings us the hurricane, the earthquake, the flood of red-hot lava rolling toward the city.

That Atlantis was one day to be destroyed was hardly any secret to me when I came here. But even so, it was a truly miserable experience to be forced to watch at close range as the news of the city's inevitable doom was brought to someone who has spent his entire life preparing to be its king.

I wish I could do something for him. But he doesn't want to talk even with me. My few attempts at making mental contact have been hurled back with furious snarls. He needs to work this thing through by himself, entirely by himself.

I suppose the Athilantans see the Anointing as a necessary part of the education of a future Grand Darionis. But to me, right now, it seems terribly cruel, a needless disillusionment. It utterly pulls the rug out from under you.

Everyone wants some way of seeing into the future, of course; but these people actually have one, and look at the damage it does. If I were going to become Grand Darionis of Athilan in a few years I'd just as soon be spared the knowledge that the whole place is fated eventually to go down the tubes regardless of anything anyone do.

I did, by the way, get your last letter just before all this happened.

I'm glad to hear you backing me up on the theory that the Athilantans came here from another world. Somebody else might just have shrugged and said that poor Roy has gone completely nuts. Instead you went and peered into Governor Sippurilayl's memories of his boyhood history lessons and found that he'd been taught the same story Ram had. Of course, that doesn't mean it's true; but I think it is, and apparently so do you. Thanks for your support. A good guy, you are. I don't need to tell you, do I, how much you mean to me, how deeply I miss you, how eager I am to see you again?

And thanks also for the revised calendar information. Using the data you sent, I was able to sit down finally and plot everything out the way I should have done a long while back. I see now that my stint in Atlantis is just about over. Six days more, maybe seven, and they'll be yanking us back to our sleeping bodies up there in Home Year. So we'll actually be together again soon. I feel good about that, you can bet. But I hate the idea of leaving Atlantis at a time like this.

My God, these have been an awful few days.

With much much love—

—Roy

□ TWELVE □

This is my last letter. We'll be home soon. In fact you won't even get to read this, because it can't possibly reach you out there in Naz Glesim before we leave. But I need to set all this down on paper anyway, just to get everything clear in my own mind. Let's pretend that you'll get it next week, although you won't, not here. But you'll be hearing it from me next week in person, up in Home Era.

The basic situation is this: I've been breaking rules again. In a big way. I'm beginning to think I'm suffering from some kind of compulsion to go against everything we were trained to do when we became time observers.

What happened was that I decided that since I've got very little time left to spend in Atlantis, I would save the city from the doom that's bearing down on it before I have to leave. That's right. All by myself I would spare this great civilization from destruction.

I don't mean that I came up with some way to defuse that volcano or to keep the earthquake from happening. All I did was go to work on Prince Ram, trying to convince him to order an evacuation to some safer place while there was still time.

I should tell you that Ram had come up out of his state of deep gloom by this point. On the fifth morning after the Rite of Anointing he awakened in a perfectly calm, cheerful mood. He prayed, he swam about eighty laps in the palace pool, he ate an enormous breakfast, he met with his father and tackled a colossal stack of official reports that needed to be scanned and approved. It was as thought the Rite of Anointing had never taken place. He was absolutely his old self again. No trace remained of the dark, bitter, agonized frame of mind that had gripped him since the day of that terrible revelation.

This is evidently a familiar pattern for the Prince. Remember how upset he was when he first found out that a "demon" was hiding in his mind? Trembling, shaking, pressing his hands violently against his head to drive me out? But then he calmed down completely. In the Labyrinth, again, he got pretty excited while he was trying to work that exorcism on me; but once he realized that he had failed to expel me, he became so cheerful and tranquil that I wasn't sure he knew I was still there. He's extremely tough and well balanced. Something strange can really get to him and shake him; but in his steady, determined way he works on it, gets control of it, regains his poise. And then everything's all right for him again.

He said to me, —*You've been very quiet lately, wizard.*

—*I didn't think you needed to hear from me. You've had enough to handle.*

—*You saw what I saw? The destruction of the city?*

—*Yes.*

—*And what do you think, wizard? You know all that is to come. Was it a true vision? Or only a bad dream, a nightmare designed to test me?*

I could have given him false consolation then, I suppose. I could have lied, and said that what he had seen was a fever dream, a fantasy, that Athilan would endure forever and a day. But I'm not much good at lying. And I knew that he wasn't looking for lies from me, or consolations, or anything else that might make him feel good for a moment at the expense of the truth.

So I said, —*The city will be destroyed, Prince.*

—*Truly.*

—*Truly, yes. In my era nothing will be remembered of it except that it once existed. And many people will think that even that is only a foolish tale.*

—*Destroyed and forgotten.*

—*Yes, Prince Ram.*

He was silent for a while. But I was monitoring the flow of his moods, and there was no return to the bleakness that had gripped him in the days just after the Rite of Anointing. He was calm. He was steady.

He said at last, —*How far in the future is the*

*time of destruction, wizard? Ten thousand years? Five
thousand?*

    —Perhaps ten thousand years. Perhaps much less.

    —Perhaps it will happen this year, even?

    —I don't know, Prince.

    —A wizard should know the future.

    *—But your calling me a wizard doesn't make me one,
Prince. What you speak of as the future is the remote and
misty past to me. I have no way of knowing when Athilan
perished. Believe me, Prince.*

    Another period of silence. Then he said:

    —I believe you—wizard.

    And then I said, taking myself completely by
surprise, *—Prince, you need to save your city while
there's still time.*

    —Save it? How could I possibly save it?

    *—Leave this island. Lead everyone across to the main-
land. Build a new Athilan in some place that will be
invulnerable. And it will endure forever.*

    I felt undertones of amazement coming from
him. I tell you, I was amazed myself at what I was
doing.

    But I couldn't help it, Lora. I was caught up in
the crazy rapture and wonder of my scheme.

    I told him where to erect his New Atlantis. *—Go
to North Africa,* I said. *It's warm there. There's a place
called Egypt, where a mighty river flows out of the heart of
the continent. Your ships can get there easily from here, by
sailing east and south. The land is fertile. You'll have
access to the sea. There's stone to build with. You can
create a new empire ten times as great as this one, one that
will spread around the world.*

—Or else, I said, *go further east, to a place known as Mesopotamia. There are two rivers there, and it's warm there too, and the land is perhaps even more fertile than in Egypt. And from there you can expand ever eastward, to a land called India, and one called China. You'll be better off there than in Europe—in the mainland right here. Europe will be locked in ice for many more thousands of years. But China—India—Egypt—*

I was berserk, Lora.

I was grossly interfering with the past. Not only had I opened direct contact with my own time-host, but here I was trying to get him to take a course of action that would beyond any doubt change the entire direction of history! Carried away by my own brilliance, I was telling him to go and found Egypt long before the Pharaohs would. Or better yet to create his new kingdom in Sumer or Babylon, and then to colonize the Orient, and—this part didn't even matter to me, so crazed was I, so eager was I to be helpful—set up a Second Athilantan Empire that might become so powerful it would last on and on right into what you and I think of as historical times!

How about that? A tremendous sprawling kingdom ruled by extraterrestrial aliens, dominating the world for the next twenty thousand years, while none of our "real" history gets a chance to occur! No Greece, no Rome, no England, no United States— only eternal Athilan, all-powerful, reaching out in every direction, controlling everything! What a vision! What lunacy, Lora!

I offered to draw maps for him. I offered to give him geographical lessons. I promised to ransack my brains for every detail of what I knew about the Palelotiic Near East.

He let me rave for a long time.

And then he said, finally, —*What a rare vision this is. What a wondrous scheme.*

—*Yes*, I said, sure that I had convinced him.

And then: —*But you know I would never do anything like this, wizard. Not even if I were Grand Darionis today, and I knew that the calamity would fall upon us in ten months' time, would I do such a thing.*

I was caught off balance.

—*You wouldn't?*

He laughed. —*Why do you think the princes of Athilan are shown the vision of the Rite of Anointing?*

I said, really flustered now —*Well—it's because—I would assume—that is, it seems to me that it's done in order to prepare you for the eruption. In case you happen to be the one who's King at the time when it actually takes place. So that you can plan to take protective measures, arrange a safe evacuation, things like that.*

—*No. Not at all.*

—*Why is it done, then?*

He paused a moment. Then he said, —*To teach us that even though we are kings, we are as nothing in the hands of the gods.*

—*I don't understand.*

—*You are no wizard then.*

—*I have never pretended to be one.*

He said, —*The gods have decreed that Athilan one day must perish, just as they decreed the fiery death of Romany Star. Don't you think that we were aware that that would happen, too? And this city came out of that* one. *New greatness flowers out of lost greatness. It is our destiny, wizard, from time to time to be chastised by the gods, to be driven forth in sorrow from our homes, to begin anew, to create that which never existed before to replace that which was taken from us. Do you think we dare defy the gods? Do you think we dare thwart their will? We must accept what comes to us. That is the lesson of the Rite of Anointing. That is the thing I had to learn, if I am to be Grand Darionis some day. The vision was a test, yes. And I have passed that test.*

—*Your ancestors knew that Romany Star would be destroyed? And they did nothing to save themselves?*

—*They built sixteen starships, and loaded aboard them whatever they could. The rest they left behind to face the flames. And when the catastrophe comes to the isle of Athilan, we will have ships ready, and once again we will save what we can. The rest will be destroyed beyond recovery.*

I said, bewildered, —*I can't believe that you'll just sit here like sheep and take no action, even though you can see the future and you know that the future holds destruction for you.*

—*Tell me this, wizard. In your era, do people still die?*

—*Yes. Of course.*

—*And yet you go about your daily lives, doing your work and making plans for the future and seeking always to better yourselves, even though you know that in twenty or thirty or fifty years you will certainly be dead? You don't simply give up and lie down, the moment you discover that death is inevitable, and abandon all striving right at that point?*

—*It isn't the same thing,* I said. *The individual has to die sooner or later, yes. But the family goes on, the nation goes on, the world goes on. Each one of us does his part in the time that's allotted. What other choice do we have?*

—*And if you knew—you absolutely knew—that the world itself would perish on the day of your own death? Would you give up all striving because it seemed futile, wizard? Or would you continue to work and plan?*

His argument seemed wrong to me. —*But this isn't a matter of the whole world being destroyed! It's a matter of one island being struck by catastrophe, and its people having advance warning of the fact, and being unwilling to move to a safer place despite everything they know. That makes no sense to me.*

—*Only the kings know of the doom that is coming. Not any other soul.*

—*Even so. If the kings know, it's their duty to save their people.*

—*And shall the king then thwart the will of the gods?* Ram asked. *We must take what comes. And fully learn the lesson the gods wish to teach.*

That was where I gave up. I understood, then: these people really are *alien.* Their minds don't work like ours. They see the steamroller coming, and they refuse to get out of the way. It's the will of the gods, they say. And for them that's all there is to it. Pure fatalism. A philosophy like that isn't easy for me to comprehend. But after all I'm only a visitor here.

And my visit's almost over. I feel the bond weakening; I feel Home Era starting to pull me back. In a little while I'll be up front there, giving my report, confessing my blatant errors of judgment, surrendering myself to the judgment that's waiting for me. If I'm lucky they'll go easy on me. I understand that I'm not the first time-traveler to give in to the temptation to help his host avoid serious trouble. We're only human, after all.

And what will happen here, I wonder?

Well, Atlantis will be destroyed. That was a given fact from the start. Perhaps it'll happen when Ram is king, perhaps in the reign of some grandchild of his—but it will happen. No question of it. Fire and brimstone will fall, and the sea will rise, and the island will be swallowed up. In that moment the empire will end.

But a few ships are going to escape. I'm certain of that.

Where will they go? Egypt? Mesopotamia?

Will they live to build still another civilization, which will eventually perish also, but manage to pass a few fragments onward, until our world, the world that we call "modern," has taken form? Somewhere in our own world today are the descendants of these Athilantans. Of that I'm certain too. These perpetual wanderers, these many-times-refugees— surely they endure, surely they still dwell among us. By now they've forgotten their own history, I suspect. They don't know that their ancestors came from another world to live among us Dirt People, and once built the greatest empire that ever was, of which not a trace remains. It's all forever lost, back here in the distant buried corridors of time.

But that's not important. Time devours everything. Entire histories vanish. What matters is en-
durance. The spirit survives and goes onward when
the palaces crumble and the kings are forgotten.

And if I've learned anything from this fantastic
journey in time, Lora, that's it. You too, out there
among the mammoth-hunters in their houses of bone,
have seen what it's like to struggle against hostile
nature and prevail. I, here in glittering Athilan, have
also discovered a thing or two about how harsh a
place the universe can be, and how stubborn we
mortals can be in fighting back.

Ram knows I'm leaving soon, disappearing into
a distant future time that's not even a dream to him.
I wonder if he'll miss his "demon," his "wizard." I
suspect he will.

I know I'm going to miss him. He's the most
noble guy I've ever known. And I think he's going
to be the greatest Grand Darionis that the Empire of
Athilan has ever had.

And that's the whole story. It's just about time
to go now, love. I'll be seeing you in a little while,
only twenty thousand years from here. I hope they
have a pizza waiting for us when we get there.